Three in the Morning

Jazzie Burgos

Ukiyoto Publishing

All global publishing rights are held by

Ukiyoto Publishing

Published in 2021

Content Copyright © **Jazzie Burgos**
ISBN 9789364941747

All rights reserved.
No part of this publication may be reproduced, transmitted, or stored in a retrieval system, in any form by any means, electronic, mechanical, photocopying, recording or otherwise, without the prior permission of the publisher.

The moral rights of the author have been asserted.

This is a work of fiction. Names, characters, businesses, places, events, locales, and incidents are either the products of the author's imagination or used in a fictitious manner. Any resemblance to actual persons, living or dead, or actual events is purely coincidental.

This book is sold subject to the condition that it shall not by way of trade or otherwise, be lent, resold, hired out or otherwise circulated, without the publisher's prior consent, in any form of binding or cover other than that in which it is published.

www.ukiyoto.com

Dedication

I dedicate this book to the strong and godly women in my life who are now enjoying heaven with Jesus, my *Lola Marina Tagle*, my *Mommy Marina Hernandez* and my beloved mother and best friend, *Mama Enriqueta Tagle-Burgos*. God used them to influence me on service, prayer, faith, love for family and reverence to God.

I also dedicate this book to all patients and students who are struggling with the storms in life and are longing to find hope in God. Most of the stories in this book are stories of my personal journey, and of people I met in the clinic, campus and church.

"Very early in the morning, while it was still dark, Jesus got up, left the house and went off to a solitary place, where He prayed."

Mark 1:35

Acknowledgements

I praise my God for all that He does and all that He is. He is my love, my life, my reason and my everything. He is my greatest Physician, Teacher and Companion, the One that I talk to every three in the morning. He is my Rock, my Savior, Redeemer and Lord, the only One that I worship and adore.

I thank my Papa Ricky for being a credible role model to me. He is also doing his devotion early in the morning. I see his faithfulness to God and to family since I was a kid. I thank my 510 family, Jeiar, Psalm, JR, Janice, Ate Jhelyn and Dhalyn, thank you for all that you do to keep the family strong through the years. I love you all. Thank you Janice Timola for being the photographer and designer of the book cover.

Thanks to Dr. Liza Divierte, Dr. Michelle Calayag, Ate Tisha Timbang, Ate Norms Madrid and Meg Isleta for your constant encouragement to express my heart and mind through writing. Thank You for investing time to listen, to pray and to care. Special thanks to Jo Anne Ruth, Roda Mae, Jhoma May, Elaine, Agnes, Shay, Yang, Wendee and Loida for being my safe place and my constants. You bring spice and add color into my used-to-be monochromatic life. You are God's gifts to me.

To my *Leadership Group*, Iya, Shiela, Ariza, Janet, Alexis and Rose, thank you for honoring God and making disciples. You spark hope in my life and in the lives of the next generation. To my *Victory Group Interns and members* then and now, I am inspired by your palpable desire to obey and abide in God. Your stories of breakthroughs inspired me to write. To my *Life groups* in the Campus, KHAS team and in Abbott office, you make me see my workplace as a home. Our time together is my breather. Let's continue to embrace, share and declare the love of Jesus to the world!

My deepest appreciation to my Kuya Emil, Ate Rina and to all who became God's instruments to disciple me since I was a kid until I became a full-fledged doctor, I am forever grateful for your patience, stubborn love and fervent prayers.

I thank God for my patients, students and workmates, you serve as mouthpieces of His Word and channels of encouragement and blessings. I am grateful to avid readers of my write ups on facebook, Instagram and my website, for all the affirmations. Thanks to my cousin, Eva Sta. Ana-Gonzales, for bridging the way for this book to be published.

My utmost gratitude to Victory Alabang Pastors and Staff and to my Every Nation Campus family for the impartations, declarations, prayers and opportunities to serve the next generation and young professionals.

I bring back all the glory and honor to the One whom all praise is due, JESUS.

Heartfelt thanks,
Jazzie

CONTENTS

Identity   *1*

My name is JACQUELINE	1
Am I not good enough?	4
Charm is deceptive	7
Straighten your crown	9
Home maker to Queen maker	12
You are a bright light	14
Mistaken Identity	17
Salt and Light	20

Strength   *23*

Strong, God-dependent woman	23
New Reasons to Run	26
I know who I am	28
Why Me?	31
Supernatural Rescue	33
There is a God of Strength	36
Give God your pain	39

Courage   *42*

Unafraid	42
Lord, make me brave	43
A Warrior is Born	45
David's Historical Win	49
The new meaning of the past	50
Courage to Move On	53

Hope   *56*

Listen, Pray and Heal	56

Hope when it hurts	58
Has life been cruel?	60
Should I thank God for delays?	63
Dream Again	66
Failure is an open door	68
The God of our waiting time	71
Need a Miracle?	73
God provides	75

Healing — *78*

Doctors also need a Healer	78
Touch His robe	80
Healing or Healer?	82
Behind the mask	85
I love you, Doc	87
Broken to whole	90
Cancer Patients	93
He puts all shackles off my feet	96
Imperfect parents	98
Lets Talk	100
Emotional Distancing	103
Status: In a relationship (for 27 years)	106
Motivated by love	108
Simple joys	111
He thinks about me	113

Devotion — *115*

Missing Piece	115
All I desire is Christ	117
Unharmed by fire	118
Doorkeeper and an empty chair	120

How do you measure love?	122
My First, My Best and My All	124
How can I not trust you, Lord?	127
We need God	128
Ultimate Source	131
Di ako aalis dito	133
About the Author	***136***

Identity

My name is JACQUELINE

My Papa and Mama got my name, JACQUELINE, from Jacqueline Kennedy Onassis because they wanted me to become rich. But honestly, I didn't like that name much because I thought it's too long and it doesn't fit my personality. I was timid when in a crowd, I had old-school fashion and I had simple dreams.

Secondly, I learned from school that Jacqueline was derived from Jacob's name which means cheater, holder of the heel (He was born holding Esau's heel) and a supplanter (he deprived his brother of his right as first born). That's why I didn't enjoy that name.

But, I love my nickname, JAZZIE. I think it's cool, classy and unique. Just like jazz music, it has no pattern but it's timeless.

In 2019, I met a car accident. My car was damaged and was 'deeply wounded'. But miraculously, I was totally unharmed. The day after that accident, God revealed to me the real meaning of my name through my mentor, Dr. Liza. She said Jacqueline (in Hebrew) means GOD PROTECTS. My sardonic self-talk was, 'Wow. Really?'. But when she began to expound more about it, I got really amused. It changed the way I valued my name.

I AM PROTECTED. The memories of those times the Lord protected me since childhood started to revisit my mind. He protected me from wrong people, decisions and choices. He sheltered me in times of need, chaos and calamities. I was accident prone as a youth. I fell from a moving bus, I fell from Han-ul San mountain in South Korea, I fell in a man hole, I slide and trip frequently. But the Lord protected me, I seldom get bruises from all those mishaps. He kept me safe from diseases, accidents and life's troubles. He guarded my fragile heart when it was about to break. God is indeed my Protector. And God also reminded me that after Jacob's encounter with Him, He changed his name to Israel which means *Triumphant with God*.

I AM A "HEEL". Though my name meant "holder of heel" and cheater, when Jesus found me, He changed the definition of 'heel' in my life. Now, when I think of HEEL, I think of strength, movement, connection and stability. It's the largest bone of all feet bones. Its unique design and structure accommodate all other bones, muscles and ligaments.

They work together for a human being to stand, to walk and to run. It makes a lot of sense now that God is allowing me to go beyond who I used to be and what I used to do. He gave me the privilege to lead students and young professionals through discipleship. God forged new and godly relationships, He invited me into a new season and opened doors for new opportunities to change the world to honor him.

I AM RICH IN GOD. My parents wanted me to become rich. God honored that desire. God has been my source of everything, supplying all my needs according to His riches in glory through Christ. I don't lack anything because He is my Shepherd. I am rich in love because my God is LOVE.

I delight in discovering the truths about my name. It brings joy to my soul and healing to my inmost being. He truly knows me by name. How about you, what is God telling you about your name?

"Behold, I have engraved your name on the palms of my hands." Isaiah 49:16

Am I not good enough?

We've never been 'locked down' this long in our lifetime. 2020 was by far the year that I had the most number of consultations that are thought to be something organic or physical, but turned out to be manifestations of anxiety, insecurity, loneliness, discouragement and hopelessness.

When people make you feel you are not worth their time and attention, how will you respond?

When spectators tell you, you are worthless if you don't achieve, how would you feel?

When circumstances make you feel you are not strong enough, what would be your action plan?

When efforts don't match with the output, what will you do?

When your good intentions and acts of kindness are misinterpreted, will you stop being kind?

When the people you chose to love didn't choose you back, will you feel unworthy?

As for me, I would believe God more than how the world or anybody else would define me.

In case no one has told you lately, let me remind you of these words...

He said,

YOU ARE WORTH MY ATTENTION

'He protected you, He cared for you, He kept you as the apple of His eye.'

He Said,

YOU ARE STRONG

'He gives power to the weak and strength to the powerless.'

He said,

YOU WILL REAP

'At just the right time we will reap a harvest of blessing if we don't give up.'

He said,

YOU ARE NOT OVERLOOKED

'He will not forget how hard you have worked for Him and how you have shown your love to him by caring for others.'

He said,

YOU ARE LOVED.

'I have loved you with an everlasting love. I have never quit loving you, Expect love, love, love and more love'

He is not looking at you from a distance.

He is the God who is WITH you.

He sees every tear and every fear.

He knows that you are tired of all the uncertainties and the lies.

He has the solution.

He will never abandon.

He calls you His own

He is a perfect God who has always strengthened you, provided for you, been patient with you, trained you for war and saved you. He went through great lengths of sacrifice to express that unparalleled love for you. People REJECT us because we are not good enough. But JESUS DIED for us because we are not good enough. We fall short of His glory.

The truth is, no one is ever enough. For all have sinned and fall short of the glory of God (Romans 3:23). Not a single person on earth has perfectly obeyed God's commandments. But Christ loved us with an everlasting love. He loved us and died for us at our ugliest, messiest and darkest.

In Him, you are precious. You are wanted. You are honored. You are greatly loved. Receive that love.

"While we were still sinners, Christ died for us."
Romans 5:8

Charm is deceptive

Men (human beings) look at outward appearance. We judge (sometimes love and accept) people based on their looks, skin color and texture, nails, hair, weight, words, loudness (or quietness), performance, titles and achievements. Our nearsightedness prevents us from seeing what really matters.

Unfortunately, we also judge ourselves just the same. We think that our worth is just on the surface. We feel insecure, unaccepted and unloved. We tell ourselves 'perhaps, someone MORE beautiful, intelligent, modest, fluent, eloquent or someone taller, leaner, fairer, smarter deserves that than me'. We forget our grandest dreams and our deepest desires, because we were deceived by the worldly view that we are not qualified. We look at the mirror and see every blemish, every flaw and every imperfection, thinking that these limitations will depreciate our value.

We tell the world, "I am secured". But when we search into the deepest creases of our hearts, we find the real score that we are swallowed and crushed by insecurities and our false and poor judgement of our very own worth and beauty. We are trapped into the thought that this world is reserved only for the rich, the intelligent and the beautiful.

CHARM is deceptive. We were blinded by what our naked eyes see. We make decisions and rule our emotions based on the lies and misconceptions about our worth. We devaluate and bully our own appearance and become amnesic on the very intention of the ONE who created us!

But you know what?

No matter how we devalued and treated ourselves, our worth will never change. Our Maker still finds us as beautiful, stunning and delightful as how He created us. Nothing less than that. He sees us as a JEWEL, a priceless TREASURE. God looks at the heart. We find our REAL BEAUTY in that heart.

He shaped you inside and out. He formed, protected, nurtured and chosen you while you were still in your mother's womb. What a breathtaking truth—- that you were marvelously made! He knows your name and your thoughts, He knows every bone, every eyebrow strand, every fiber and every cell in your body; He knows exactly how you were carved from nothing into something. He watched you grow from conception to birth; all the stages of your life were spread out before His eyes.

The world's view on beauty is weak and shallow. Superficial beauty is fleeting and vain. Your real beauty is your character. The very character of Jesus manifested in your life. A woman who fears the LORD... reverently worshiping, obeying, serving, and trusting Him with awe-filled respect, shall be praised.

"I praise You because of the wonderful way you created me.

Everything you do is marvelous! I know that full well." Psalms 139:14

Straighten your crown

Remember the movie, Princess Diaries? A shy, clumsy 15 year-old learned one day that her dad is a son of a queen which made her a real Princess.

Same with us, when we became believers of Christ, we became heirs of God. We became sons and daughters of the King of kings, our self-concept suddenly CHANGED. There was a change in mind set, perspective and vision. There was a new reason why we exist and a change in the way we live. However, the process is not abrupt. It's a daily process of pruning, shaping, refining and reminding.

And as we are slowly being molded and trained to be the kind of 'PRINCESS' that the Lord designed us to be, we also speak, think and act based on our identity. We start to speak life and blessing; we fix our thoughts on what are true, honorable, right, pure, lovely, admirable, excellent and worthy of praise. We deal with things with Kingdom mindset based on what His Word says. We act justly, love mercy and walk humbly. We improve ourselves, we overlook offenses and fix our eyes on what really matters because we know that all these things honor our Father in heaven. From an unnoticed nobody, even without pushing, we turn into a somebody who impacts our family, our campus, our workplace and the society.

But we still live in a broken world.

We still have troubles, emotions and crossroads. We go through storms and face big mountains. We walk through valleys of weeping and dark nights. People will remind us of our past. We receive unsolicited criticisms, experience humiliations, and worse, face situations that threaten our faith and hope. Unknowingly, our pain and suffering blur and shift our vision from our mighty God to our overwhelming troubles.

We get swallowed and driven by our emotions. We get confused when we reach our crossroads. Realizing our inadequacies, limitations and lack of control often lead us to fear, retaliation, desensitization and neglect. This internal chaos prowl like roaring lions looking for someone to devour. It attempts to snatch our joy and peace. It seeks out to drop our crown! Be alert and of sober mind!

Know that the purpose of every circumstance is for us to seek after God, feel our way towards Him and find Him. Do not allow harsh circumstances to bring out the person that we are not. Our pain may sometimes mask the truth and our real identity. But let your faith and your allegiance to God unleash the warrior, the worshipper, the artist, the wise, the beautiful PRINCESS in you.

"REMEMBER WHO YOU ARE". That is what King Mufasa told his successor, SIMBA, to remind him of what he is made of… "You are my son and the one true king!" (Lion King). So when you think of how fragile, inadequate, imperfect, forgotten, despicable, worthless and helpless you are, remember who you really are, the you are the DAUGHTER of the KING.

C'mon Woman of God, straighten your CROWN!

"So you are no longer a slave, but God's child; and since you are his child,

God has made you also an heir." Galatians 4:7

Home maker to Queen maker

Many of my friends thought that all I want in life is to study and build my career. Haha! They're wrong!

Since highschool, whenever asked what I want to be, I would always answer, "I want to be a Home Maker". I've always been inspired with wives/moms who design their homes, cook for their family, tutor their children, braid their daughter's hair, landscape their garden and drive their children to school. I love seeing women who are raising godly children, teaching them the bible, praying with them, playing with them, singing them lullaby before bedtime, doing household chores and doing ministry and mission with their husbands. Oh what a beautiful picture!

I love conversations with mothers.

I know God is taking his time in every season. While I am not a home maker yet, I know God has a great work for me to do as a single person. Something like what Mordecai did in the life of Queen Esther.

When Esther's parents died, he adopted her and raised her as his own daughter, gave wise advice and taught her integrity. When Esther was in the palace, Mordecai encouraged her to go to the king on behalf of the people. This would have meant that he could potentially have lost Esther, as this would risk her life. However, he must have been prepared to COUNT THE COST for the sake of the mission for the people. He raised and trained Esther to be the *most qualified queen*. Esther was not only innately beautiful, but Mordecai established her inner strength that made her do the right thing when given that moment to alter the circumstances. She took courage to save the people. Mordecai and Esther fasted together as they faced that very critical moment of talking to the king.

Single women, this is our season to hone and teach the next generation. Not only academically but emotionally, socially, mentally and most importantly, spiritually. We may not be queens or homemakers of any household right now, but the Lord gave us people to take care of and to love as our very own children. As a physician and an educator, I find great honor in raising future doctors, leaders and world changers! This opportunity is something that I love to embrace... a chance to be a QUEEN MAKER like Mordecai.

'And David shepherded them with integrity of heart; with skillful hands he led them.' Psalm 78:72

You are a bright light

When we experience fiascos and disasters, and when we fail to meet the standards of what we are expected to do, unknowingly, our self-concept also changes.

From 'I can' to 'I can't'
From 'I will be' to 'I won't be'

Been through many versions of that before. I disappointed everyone when I almost got kicked out in high School, didn't had a good start in med school, had failed relationships (and friendships) and was not a good steward of my blessings. After those traumatic seasons, I recovered but I felt I will always fail on everything I will do.

On top of that, I had a low self-esteem and I thought nobody wanted to be like me. I was timid, boring and passive and I thought there was nothing exciting about my life. I was convinced that it's better for me to just be a lone ranger than to feel rejected by others. I was comfortable managing and accomplishing things alone.

But my perspective changed when I started to take God's word seriously. By reading His word, I realized that all I was thinking about myself was a misconception. Out of obedience to God, I decided to get out of my lonely comfort zone and dared to start connecting with people. I took courage to let go of my 'failure-mentality'.

After few months, I saw myself already working with several people: students, patients, old and new friends, officemates and churchmates. I never thought that God will use my (several) stories of failures to lift others up and help them see that there is HOPE. I didn't know that God can use my seasons of loneliness to understand and uplift those who are currently losing their self-esteem and fervor in moving forward. I woke up one day realizing that God already turned my mourning into dancing, my sorrows into joy and my darkness into light... hmmm, INTO A BRIGHT LIGHT. This light illuminates in the darkness because it's the light of Jesus!

I am convinced that it is not one's success, wealth nor fame that will make his life shine. Rather, it is God's stories of redemption and transformation that will make it shine even BRIGHTER.

This light will draw people to Christ and make them glorify our Father in heaven. Shine on!!

"In similar way, let your light shine before others, that they may see your good deeds and glorify your Father in heaven."
Matthew 5:16

Mistaken Identity

The nature of man produces depression, anxiety and stress (including rage, violence, anger, filthy speech, quarrel, corruption). The nature of man is the FRUIT of being in a broken, self-centered and sinful world. The world's definition of man is based on the struggles we go through while living in a wrecked world.

But the design of man is different. The design of man is the WHY behind the what. It is the original intention of our Maker in creating us and the real purposes why we exists. It answers the question: Why on earth am I here for?

Genesis 1 redefined the concept of Man in my heart. The design of man is to reflect and mirror his Maker. We have the same physical, mental and moral attributes; created for stability, uniqueness, greatness, growth, purpose, magnificence, creativity and newness. We have that wondrous ability to build, connect, think, reason, flourish, love, reflect and honor God. These are His purpose for creating Man.

However, because of the disobedience of the parents of the human race (Adam and Eve), the godly and perfectly designed man was broken. We have forgotten our image and design. This world slowly turned into a place filled with uncertainties and lies, it became broken due to sin.

But broken mirrors, still reflects, right? We still have that image. But it needs fixing and reconstruction (not just repair). Doctors, mentors and scientists can attempt to fix it. But only our Maker can restore it.

The world says, "you need to perform",

> the Lord says, "trust in Me".

The world says, "beauty means perfection"

> the Lord says, "beauty means a gentle and quiet spirit".

The world says, "you are a failure"

> the Lord says, "I will make you surefooted as a deer".

The world says, "you are born to compare"

> the Lord says, "you are wonderfully complex".

The world says, "you are alone"

> the Lord says, "you can never get away from My presence".

The world says, "failure is fatal"

> the Lord says, "I will restore you and make you strong, firm and steadfast".

The world says, "your worth is on your work"

> the Lord says, "I chose you before I gave you life".

The world says, "follow your heart"

> the Lord says, "your heart and your strength fail, but I am the strength of your heart.".

The world says, "God is impersonal and unreal"

> the Lord says, "I go before you and follow you. I am with you".

The world says, "God is watching us from a distance"

> the Lord says, "My nearness of you is your good".

I personally believe that anxiety, depression, distress, insecurity, loneliness and hopelessness are not just caused by imbalances of chemicals in the body but an issue of forgetfulness. We have forgotten whose sons and daughters we are. We are created after God's own image, we inherit His mind and heart, we are meant for greatness, we are victorious, our future is sure and secure. We are precious. We are never forgotten. We are strong and we can soar on wings like eagles.

When we look at the world, all we see is a hopeless end. But when we look at Jesus, we only see an endless hope. We have a perfect FATHER who has always loved us, He gave His only Son that whoever believes in Him shall not perish but have an eternal life. Jesus went to great and extreme sacrifice to express that love for you.

"Do not fear, for I have redeemed you; I have summoned you by name; you are mine."
Isaiah 43:1

Salt and Light

What does it mean to be SALT and LIGHT?

Just like Salt that creates thirst and attracts water. People are drawn to you because they see that there is something in you that gives them strength and hope. You add value to people, you build and enrich relationships, and You speak with wisdom.

You are the SALT that enhances flavor to wherever God has called you. You make them see the purpose why they study, why they work, why they serve and why they live. God uses you, to be a channel of inspiration, and healing to the poor and broken hearted, because your life reflects the very character of Jesus. You are the salt—the preserving influence in this world. God uses you to stop the progressive moral and spiritual decay by promoting righteousness and living a God-honoring life.

You are the light of the world that shines to dispel darkness. That's why you work skillfully and excellently with integrity. Excellence is an expression of the nature of the great and marvelous God who is enthroned in our hearts. It manifests from heart to hands, from the inside out, from root to fruit, from holiness to fruitfulness. We manifest the mind of Christ and His true character by living a life worthy of Him.

You are the best person to be the salt and light in your family, in your campus, in your workplace and in your society. The light that we illuminate comes from the ultimate light of the world, Jesus.

God uses our bright light to change the world, to share the salvation and love of Christ and to spread the truth that Only Him can give meaning to our lives and turn our darkness into light

Matthew 5:13-16, it tells us, that we are the salt of the earth and the light of the world. We are commanded to let our light shine before others, so that they may see your good works and give glory to your Father who is in heaven.

Strength

Strong, God-dependent woman

I studied for a total of 32 years from nursery to medicine then Masters and PhD. During my first 10 years as a doctor, I was also teaching while juggling 5 more jobs. People always thinks I am a strong woman. They said I never looked helpless. They didn't know I've been tired all my life… tired of thinking, planning, meeting expectations and problem solving. I felt obliged to look strong even when I was not. People didn't see how I wished people would do to me the things I do for them. I seldom asked help because of fear of rejection and frustration. I understood then that physical weariness is far better than mental and emotional exhaustion.

But God used a stranger named Meg to shatter all the lies I used to believe. She encouraged me to speak out my self-talk, we processed and prayed about every issue and every detail. Our coffee shop meet-ups became a safe place. She went beyond listening, she exerted 200% effort to help me find my way out of the maze I was trudging. She constantly pushed me back to Jesus and draw strength from Him alone.

Human strength is naturally limited. It wears out. It's natural to get tired. But let me share with you some of the things I learned in the past 6 years,

1. Learn to pause and rest. Physical weariness is resolved by slowing down and by sleep. Simple.
2. Learn to ask help from people around you. What an irony that people need help, but never ask for help. Never confuse strength with pride. Never think that you are the only one who is able and available to offer help. Receiving help is as important as offering help. No man is an island. God will bring you people to journey with you.
3. Learn to find strength from God. No amount of sleep can cure an emotionally and spiritually tired person. God's strength is supernatural. Blessed are those whose strength is from the Lord. When they walk through the Valley of Weeping, it will become a place of refreshing springs. They become stronger as the days pass by, as the mountain gets higher, as the waves get bigger and as the storm rages more ferociously. That is God's strength! It's PERFECT in our weaknesses.

Outwardly we are wasting away but inwardly, we are being renewed day by day. Our strength will be something that people will look up to. People who are broken will be drawn and encouraged. This strength will be passed on to the next generations. It will enlighten, inspire and motivate them to excel and win in life. The memories of our journey will keep their fire burning and will keep their hope alive.

It is only when we TRUST GOD that we find NEW STRENGTH. His strength alone can make us soar higher above the thermals of the earth. It will make us run and win the race.

As what an old song says,

"His strength is perfect when our strength is gone

He'll carry us when we can't carry on

Raised in His power, the weak becomes strong

His strength is perfect.

His strength is perfect…

God's perfect strength changed how I view myself from being a 'strong, independent woman' in to a 'strong, God-dependent woman'.

"But those who hope in the Lord will renew their strength. They will soar on wings like eagles; they will run and not grow weary, they will walk and not be faint."

Isaiah 40:31

New Reasons to Run

When my Mom passed away in 2019, I became reluctant and complacent. I lost fervor in doing the things I used to love doing: work and ministry. I felt exhausted even at rest. I wanted to relocate and change career. I wanted to cry and exercise my right to grieve. I wanted to isolate and talk to no one.

I was overthinking the impulsive options I had in mind.

But one day, God reminded me of my patients and my students. I can't understand why that thought renewed my enthusiasm in an instant. This verse spoke to my heart and gave me new reasons to go back on track:

"He took David from tending the ewes and lambs and made him the shepherd of Jacob's descendants

— God's own people, Israel. David shepherded them with a heart of integrity and unselfish devotion; he led them with the skill of his hands."

Psalms 78:72

It gave me renewed strength. It made me understand that sometimes, even though we think that the waves before us are too big, the load behind us are too heavy and the battles we face are too impossible to conquer, God will not allow us to let go and give up.

In our agony, God's solution is not isolation but solitude.

In our grief, God brings joy as we choose to refresh others.

In our frailty, God gives strength as we comfort and speak life to others.

In our failure, God uses us to lift others up.

In our pain, He will allow us to heal the wounds of our friends.

In our hunger, He will fill us by feeding others.

In our distress, He will ask us to comfort our neighbors.

In our fear, He will compel us to encourage and inspire.

In our hopelessness, He will renew our hope by reminding others of endless hope in Christ.

In our darkest moments, He will give us courage to walk by faith… and when we look behind us, we see people who used to be in darkness but has found light while following our footsteps.

In those difficult moments, God is making His light shine through us.

He will never get tired of giving us new reasons to embrace the pain and new strength to run the race.

I know who I am

I was raised to believe that I was a warrior, a tiger sister, a woman with an iron heart who was too courageous to face all kinds of battles and challenges, who never feared to be alone and cannot be threatened to be defeated. I was somebody who never looked unguarded and was always determined to finish every race STRONG!

But my own storms uncovered that behind my sturdy countenance, there was emptiness. I felt weary, weak, anxious, worn-out, drained and wrecked. My 'fight and flight' mode outwardly was a 'weak and feeble' heart inwardly. As I pour out my heart before the Lord, He didn't give me instant strength and courage. Instead, He gave me peace. He made me feel that there is nothing to prove and that He wanted me to be completely dependent on Him. I felt relief despite all the chaos and dangers I was facing. I have proven that I was not born strong. My strength doesn't come from me. Rather, I was made strong. My strength comes from the One who gives power to the weary and the lame; the One that renews the strength of our shaky arms and tired knees.

I found honor in confessing that I was a wounded warrior whose wounds were healed by the Wonderful Counselor and Mighty God. I am a woman whose heart was made whole after being crashed and whose shattered life is now filled with love, grace and mercy. I was made to worship God and manifest His strength in me.

I no longer see myself as a tiger sister nor a woman with an iron heart.

I know who I really am.

I am a child of God. I have been bought with a price.

I belong to God. I have been redeemed and forgiven of all my sins

I have been filled in Christ and I am complete in Him.

I cannot be separated from His love.

I am confident that the good work that God has began in me will be completed.

I was not given a spirit of fear, but of power, love and self-control.

I am God's workmanship. I can do all things through Christ who strengthens me.

I believe I am blessed beyond measure. By His strength alone, I overcome.

My source of strength is CHRIST ALONE.

"For when I am weak, then I am strong." 2 Corinthians 12:10

Why Me?

When faced with big opportunities and great tasks, it is inevitable for us to ask "Why me Lord? There are a lot more adequate and experienced options out there. WHO AM I to be entrusted with these tasks?

One night I prayed "I am unworthy to do these. You know my inmost being, my past, my thoughts, my secrets, pretensions and tendencies. You know my shortcomings and weaknesses. You saw how clumsy I am and how messy my life was!"

But as I slowly turned my eyes from myself to God, He changed my heart and my prayer.

When we start to fix our eyes on the Lord, we will realize that no one is righteous and deserving to serve Him. But because of His great love, He redeemed us. He gathered all the ugly and useless fragments of our hearts, He mended all the pieces of our broken lives to purify it and make it entirely His.

Who am I to be chosen to do such big tasks? I am no one. But because of God's great love and grace, I am now someone precious, rare and priceless. I am a child and a servant of God, an heir of His Kingdom, a bearer of His name. I am an ambassador of Christ.

I will tell others about His salvation, goodness and faithfulness.

And even though I am weak, He chose me and appointed me to bear fruits that will last. He gave me life, strength and victory.

"You did not choose me, but I chose you and appointed you so that you might go

and bear fruit—fruit that will last—" John 15: 16

Supernatural Rescue

A close friend asked me yesterday, "How can you manage everything?". I paused for a while and asked myself, "Am I really the one managing everything?"

Every time I go through crossroads and seasons of 'impossible', painful and difficult journey, I always ask myself, "Can I make it?" Especially when the situations are really beyond my control, wisdom and capabilities. When I realize how weak, fragile, coward, unstructured and easily distracted I am, I know in my heart, that I cannot accomplish anything and cannot make any step forward apart from a supernatural intervention.

This supernatural RESCUE has always been GOD and God alone.

Jesus rescued the demon-possessed man from unclean spirits.

Jesus rescued Peter when he began to sink on the water.

Jehoshaphat was rescued from the attack of 3 battalions of enemies.

Mordecai was rescued from the plans of Haman.

The Lord parted the Red Sea to rescue the Israelites from the Egyptians.

Jonah was rescued from the big fish.

Noah was rescued from the fatal storm and flood.
Daniel was rescued from the hungry lions in the den.

His friend were rescued from the blazing furnace.

Are you looking for someone to rescue you from your own "blazing furnace"?

When life or circumstances threaten to hurt or break you, this what the Sovereign Lord says, "I myself will search for my sheep… I will rescue them from all the places where they were scattered" (Ezekiel 34:11–12). God is your ultimate rescuer. He can take you from your miry clay.

In Jesus, there is a way out!

Sin created an immeasurable gap separating God and man, a gap that only a righteous man can bridge. No human was qualified, none of us is righteous. We all fall short of the glory of God. The wages of sin is death, but the gift of God is eternal life through Christ Jesus alone. Only Jesus could fulfill the requirement to save and rescue mankind: He is a perfect God and a perfectly sinless man. He volunteered to come to this evil world, lived the life that we should have lived and died the death that we should have died – in our place. He went into great lengths of sacrifice to express His great love for us. Three days later He rose from the dead, proving that He is the Son of God and offering the gift of salvation and forgiveness of sins to anyone who repents and believes in Him.

Jesus is the ONLY WAY out of our hopeless situation.

Surrender your life to Him, receive Him as your personal Lord and only SAVIOR. Accept Him as your ultimate RESCUER. Receive the free gift of eternal life that He is offering you. Experience a life of freedom in Him. Experience Him from the most mundane routines of daily living to the most perilous moments in our lives.

If you want to experience this supernatural rescue, pray this prayer of salvation from your heart:

Heavenly Father, I know that the gap between us is because of my sin. I admit that I have hurt You and have sinned against You. I have fallen short of Your glory. Forgive me from all my sins and cleanse me from all unrighteousness. Thank You for sending Your only Son, Jesus to die on the cross to pay for my sin. I turn my back from all sins and I receive Jesus as my only Lord and Savior. Give me grace to a life worthy of You as long as I live. I receive the gift of salvation and eternal life. In Jesus' name, Amen.

Your personal relationship with Jesus is the only way to real freedom.

"Whom the Son sets free, is free indeed!" John 8:36

There is a God of Strength

The passing of my Mom was by far the saddest and loneliest time of my life. No words of comfort were enough to silence the grief deep inside me. No place can equal the joy of sitting beside my mother, enjoying the privilege of being her daughter. The pain was persistent and doesn't go away. My eyebags don't heal because I was literally crying every day. There were days that I long to hug my Mama and tell her the best and worst parts of my day. The reality that it will never be possible to touch and see her again here on earth, paralyzes me from within.

People say, just pray. I said, it's better said than done. Even praying that time was difficult, not because of lack of faith but because the pain cannot be easily translated into words. But I realized that prayer is not about beautifully crafted words and voice dynamics. Prayer is literally pouring out your heart to God, unfiltered. That became my sweet escape in those seasons of mourning.

God's presence became the fortress that hid me from the dangers of my valleys of grieving and turned it into refreshing springs that quenched my thirst for someone I really love. It saved my life from a total wreck. His presence became heaven to me. It gave my eyes a clear picture of how Mama's death was actually God's greatest answer to my prayer for complete healing. It gave my tired hands the strength to take a new grip of the brand-new things that He has prepared for me in this new season: new places to go to, new relationships, new dreams, new direction and new mission to embrace. It gave my tired knees the strength to climb on steep mountains without stumbling. It gave my heart real joy to refresh and inspire others despite the penetrating emotional pain I was feeling. It gave me peace that God is ENOUGH.

I am confident that Mama is enjoying heaven. Day after day, God has been teaching me the very essence of trust, an all-out abandon and reckless surrender. Even if everything is falling out of place, He is reminding me that this is just His way of making things fall into His own divine order.

Indeed, behind every strong Christian is a faithful God, a Shepherd who nurtures and provides all we need. How pleasant it is to gaze upon His beauty, delighting in His glory and meditating on His word day and night.

His presence gives rock-hard comfort in our deepest pain, fear and sadness. In times when we thought we are journeying alone and no one hears our cries, remember that there is our FATHER in heaven who never leaves, will never forsake and doesn't forget. He is the Father who kisses us a thousand times when we are in pain and carries us when we are broken. He keeps us in His arms until we are ready to fly again.

MY GOD IS THE GOD OF STRENGTH. The nearness of Him is my good. He is my refuge and I will keep telling the world of His glorious and awesome works.

"Blessed are those whose strength is in you,
  in whose heart are the highways to Zion.
As they go through the Valley of Baca
they make it a place of springs;

the early rain also covers it with pools.
They go from strength to strength;
each one appears before God in Zion."

Psalms 84: 5-7

Give God your pain

I meet hurting people in school, in the office, in the hospital, at home and even online. I also experience hurtful situations. The pain lingers, not because we refuse to release it, but because sometimes, it is meant to be there for a little while.

There are circumstances that are beyond our control. Like it or not, pain will come knocking at your door in some way, shape, or form. We can try to turn it away, but pain will come in anyway. We have a choice as to how we will deal with it.

You can take two people, put them in the same difficult situation: one of them is devastated while the other demonstrates a sweet spirit.
What makes the difference? Perhaps one of them is succumbed by pain, while the other is relying in the sustaining grace of God. We can either waste our pain, or we can use it for God's glory.

When we approach God and surrender to Him, grudges, regrets, sorrows and anguish are released. As you empty your heart before the Lord, He fills that space with more of Him. It's like a barter. You give God your pain, and He will replace that with healing, joy, purpose and peace in His presence. Give God your fear, He will replace it with faith. Give God your sins, He will purify you. Give God your torn life, He will give you a new heart.

Paul gives us a great example of this in 2 Corinthians. Three times he said, "Lord, take this pain out of my life," and God didn't do it. The Bible says God's response was,

"My grace is all you need, for my power is greatest when you are weak" (2 Corinthians 12:9)

When we pray for God's help during a crisis, He will respond in one of two ways. He'll either remove the pain, or He'll give us the strength to deal with it. We don't tend to like the second option. We want God to instantly remove whatever pain we're dealing with.

When God's grace meets you in the deepest, darkest places of your life, you realize that nothing — no problem, no crisis, no hurt — can devastate your life.

You know that you can handle anything with God's help.

There is PEACE— that no matter how painful it is to go through these hurtful situations, the trouble will end. He makes all things beautiful in His time. This pain will bring out the best in you, let it serve its purpose. God has promised that He will never leave, He is mighty to save; and He is Sovereign.

Courage

Unafraid

Cast your burdens to the Lord
   And He will take care of you.
      He will never let the righteous to slip and fall.
As for me, I will call upon God
And the Lord will rescue me
Morning, noon and night
I cry out in distress
And the Lord heard my voice.
He kept track of my sorrows
And collected all my tears in His bottle
I hid beneath the shadows of His wings
Until the danger passed by
I know God is on my side
My God sent forth His unfailing love and faithfulness.
My strength is in my faith
He holds my right hand

I trusted Him over and over

Until I boldly proclaimed,
"My heart is CONFIDENT in You, God
No wonder I can sing your praises."
Psalm 57:7

Lord, make me brave

This world is full of troubles. We solve problems one after the other. We put our best effort in order to bear good fruits, but sometimes, the results remain unfavorable. We hope for a miracle but in contrary, the situation is getting worse. Bad news keeps getting you down. You choose to believe that things will still turn out great despite all the discouragements, but the circumstances seem to prove that the way to go is to give up.

How do we respond to these?

When I am faced with these kinds of situations, I lock myself inside my room to breathe and tell God, "Lord, make me brave." To acknowledge our weakness is to allow the Lord to take His place of being the sole source of all the strength that we need. Every single time I plead God to make me brave, He readily provides peace and assurance that the battle has already been won and It's a done deal. Sometimes, we just need to go through it, but the assurance of victory is there! His word tells us to take heart, be strong and courageous, not because we are innately strong, but because the One who leads the battle is STRONG. Those who trust in Him will never grow tired and weary.

Are you facing impossible situations right now,

Are you sick and the doctor said you are not responding well with the medications and now have a slim chance to survive?

Do you have a loved one who is deliberately destroying his life and is not willing to fix it?

Are you jobless and can't find a decent job that will at least provide the basic needs of your family?

Is your family falling apart and no one is willing to reconcile?

Are your grades too low and your teachers are inconsiderate?

Are you at the verge of losing your job because of relational and administrative issues?

Are you so frustrated with yourself because no matter how you try to avoid sin, you still yearn to do it and you think, you are a hopeless case?

Ask God NOW to make you brave to face these battles. He will strengthen you, rescue you and deliver you from all your enemies. He will be faithful to sustain you, protect you and carry you.

He is the God of strength and courage. He will not let you fall.

"Because you love Me, I will rescue you. I will protect you because you know My name."
Psalm 91:14

A Warrior is Born

This is one of those rare moments
That I found great joy on saying 'goodbye' permanently,
I found peace on the kind of 'ending' I used to hate
I felt relief on 'losing'
And cherished my worth by 'letting go'

I saw a brighter future on a 'closed door'

I was calm upon confirming a 'disappointing' truth
I embraced grace on 'desperation'
And prized 'leaving' as the most rewarding decision I've made.

I have found treasure in 'nothingness'
And honor on becoming weak
I found a crown after being crashed
I felt blessed after a season of brokenness

I was filled with courage to face the giant 'alone'
I was not afraid to 'stop' and 'detour' to an unfamiliar road
I found a still point in a raging wave

I found my identity while going through a 'perfect storm'.

I just stripped off that shackle that slowed me down!
I am amazingly delighted with my decision.

No turning back.

This is the day that the Lord has made, I will rejoice and be glad in it.

Today, a warrior is born.

*"The L*ORD *gave, and the L*ORD *has taken away; blessed be the name of the L*ORD*." Job 1:21*

Have you ever been an UNDERDOG?

Have you ever been part of the minority and the risk of losing is greater than the possibility of winning? How did you respond? I felt that many times! I was often placed on the side of the ring that has the most reasons to quit than to fight.

I really wanted to have my post graduate internship in the a big hospital in Manila but I had a bad start in medical school, I was not in the honor list, I had no extra-curricular involvement and I was not endorsed. I wasn't even on the list of interviewees. I took the risk and walked in. Thankfully, I was permitted to be interviewed. I was asked several questions, but this one is my favorite, "we have a lot of indigent patients here. Given a chance, are you willing to shoulder some of their laboratory expenses and medications when necessary?". My Ms. Universe answer was, "My parents are part of the middle class. But growing up, I saw them helping other people and doing community work, I think that won't be a big adjustment for me sir". To my surprise, I was accepted!

In the bible, Jehoshaphat is one of my most admired warriors. As the massive army marched towards him, Jehoshaphat fearfully acknowledged that he had no strategy to face the 3 large armies that are about to attack them! Frightened, he decided to seek the Lord's help. The Lord made an unforgettable story of victory by making them win without even fighting the way they were trained as warriors. Instead of fighting with swords, they sang worship songs, took their position and 'watched' the Lord set ambush against the men of Ammon, Moab and Mount Seir. In Jehoshaphat's desperation, He fully trusted and obeyed God no matter how unconventional the instructions were.

With God, you are a majority. Listen carefully to His instruction. He will show you the best pathway of your life. And when He says something, do not hesitate to obey. Some trusts in chariots, some trusts in horses but we boast in the name of the Lord our God. We are not afraid to fight even we look powerless and hopeless because the battle is the Lord's.

In God, you are a WARRIOR, not a worrier.

You are a VICTOR, not a victim.

You are FEARLESS, not faithless.

"For we have no power to face this vast army that is attacking us. We do not know what to do, but our eyes are on you."

2 Chronicles 20:12

David's Historical Win

How God chooses people?

Recently, I was faced with several big tasks that I thought were too heavy for me. The Lord has been comforting me through His word day after day.

In our company's national conference last 2018, during our business meeting, our big boss used David and Goliath story as an illustration.

She said, David was not chosen because of his weapon (sling and stone) but because of His courageous heart that desires nothing but to defend their territory and honor God. Secondly, he was the only one who was willing to be sent. The same courageous spirit paved the way to his historical victory.

Many times, we think that the mountains before us are too impossible to conquer. We think we're too small to face the giants. We look at our credentials and realize that we don't have the edge to win. David was a shepherd and Goliath was a warrior. David was a youth and Goliath was a giant trained for war.

But David's courage and willingness to be sent made a lot of difference. God called him to fight and blessed him with fine-tuned, high resolution vision and focus, that directed his stone to Goliath's forehead.

It's not the gear, not the position, nor the profession that mattered in this face off, but David's willingness to step forward in obedience to the call. He was not afraid because there is a greater purpose why He needed to win the fight: and that was to save his country. His purpose was greater than His fears. He did not fix his eyes on the size and threats of Goliath but to the power and greatness of His God who appointed and chosen him. David was aware of Goliath's might, but he focused on the power of God.

"David added, 'The LORD, who delivered me from the claws of the lion and the bear, will deliver me from the hand of this Philistine.' 'Go,' said Saul, 'and may the LORD be with you'."
1 Samuel 17:37

The new meaning of the past

The enemy has the habit of reminding you of your past.

What is in your past?

Failures, pains, sorrows, ungodly ways, wrong decisions, rejections, sins, guilt, shame, wounds, regrets, insecurities, identity crisis, weaknesses, soft spots, triggers, bad attitude, addiction and assaults, including those people who maligned you, hurt you, left you and spoken curses on you?

Name it. God knows it. He can change the meaning of your past.

In times that you are reminded of who you were before, TURN YOUR EYES TO GOD.
Fix it there.
Gaze upon His beauty.
Meditate on His truths.

Make His presence your home.
Delight in His perfections and hear Him tell you who you really are.

He said in His word, "The old has gone…"

He has already healed you from that.
Keep the memories of your past behind.
You are no longer who you used to be.
He said, "The new has come."
You were made new

You were made whole!

He sees you as a person who is part of His workforce.

You are a conqueror.
You are an heir.
He calls you 'friend'
He calls you 'my beloved.'

He sees you as a person of strength, power and influence.
He sees you as a warrior and a world changer.
God already changed the meaning of your past. Your past is toothless and powerless. It will never paralyze you ever again. That dark past is no longer seen as a tragedy, but a strategy that revealed God's glory. Your painful past is nothing compared to what God is going to do.

It is TIME to CHANGE the way you see things. Stop looking back! You're not going there. Do not participate in the enemy's delaying tactics. Instead, fix your eyes on Jesus, the healer of your wounds! He already took away your heart of stone and replaced it with a pristine heart of flesh.

Stand up and WALK! Do it now. It cannot wait. It's urgent. He is about to do brand-new things for you. He has already begun! He is making a pathway through the wilderness and creating rivers in the dry wasteland.

Therefore, if anyone is in Christ, this person is a new creation;

the old things passed away; behold, new things have come. 2 Corinthians 5:17

Courage to Move On

If there is ONE DAY that I wanted to erase in my memory, it is the day WHEN MY MOM LEFT US. It was just so painful.

But God has been gracious.

He was there while we were going though indescribable pain,

while we were waiting for the pain to stop lingering,

while our minds were wandering how 'the rest of our lives' will be without a mother.

while it was so hard to wake up, to work, to laugh and to go back to our usual routine;

while it's painful to go to places we usually go to (including church),

while it was a struggle to see patients with the same disease,

while I can't release the words, "I am okay".

while it was difficult to cope and to accept that the new normal is without her.

But indeed, our pains and healing are both meant for us to find our way towards God; for us to seek Him, find Him, honor Him and glorify Him. Talking to God moment by moment in my season of grieving has been my fortress of healing.

He made me fix my eyes on the reality of heaven which silenced my painful realities on earth. The time when Mama finally received her glorious miracle of healing is now something that I LOVE TO REMEMBER.
Eternal life made a lot of sense now. Because of Jesus' finished work on the cross, I am certain that my Mama is now dancing in streets of gold and worshipping our Creator face to face in heaven.

That in itself healed me and gave me courage to go back to work and share the love of Jesus to people who doesn't know Him yet.

The PAIN IS REAL. I miss Mama every single day. I still cry when I miss her. I miss her very presence and everything about her. I will forever thank the Lord for giving us a godly mother who loves Jesus more than anyone else; the mom who spent her lifetime serving, praying and loving people. The memories of her wisdom, laughter, legacies, prayers, unconditional love and faith in God are so alive in my heart. I will love her for the rest of my life. Mama has fought a good fight, she has finished her race, kept her faith and left such a godly legacy to us, her children.

As for me, I will move ahead to run my own race, to live for my purpose and to fight a good fight of faith. The Lord is my Shepherd, I have all that I need. He is far more than everything that my Mom is to me. He is with me yesterday, today and forever. Where He is, is where I want to be.

"The Lord is near to the brokenhearted and saves the crushed in spirit."

Psalms 34:18

Hope

Listen, Pray and Heal

A 35 kg Patient came in due hair loss, skin dryness, irregular menstruation, body pains, insomnia, and tingling sensation. She was seeking for nutritional advise. Her lips were smiling but her eyes didn't. I knew right away that nutrition is not her major problem. It's something else.

After the consultation, I asked her, "*kamusta ka ba?* How can i pray for you?"

Her smiling lips suddenly shifted to real sadness. She began to cry and started to pour out. She said that she has been hopping from one doctor to another, she went to different specialists and subspecialists from different hospitals. She has been through many laboratory tests and scans, but no diagnosis has been confirmed.

She shared that she has been depressed since high school (she's on her early 30s) and it keeps coming back when there are triggers. She appreciated our time so much and said that that was the first time that someone took time to hear her out.

We talked about her condition; I gave her referral letters and practical advice; we declared scriptures about hope, peace, joy and God's love and then we prayed.

Depression is a state that is marked by feelings of low self-worth or guilt, extreme feeling of sadness and a reduced ability to enjoy life. Depression should not be taken for granted. There are physical manifestations that probably mask your real emotional condition. Please do not deal with it alone. Share it with your family, a close friend, your doctor, teacher, pastor or whoever trusted person you think can support you. Hold on to the God who will never leave you nor forsake you. He is the source of your joy, peace and comfort.

God encourage you and show you that there is HOPE.

When the cares of my heart are many, your consolations cheer my soul.

Psalm 94:19

Hope when it hurts

Challenges are not meant to make us suffer and be deprived of the things that we think we deserve to have. These trials happen for our good because we know that suffering produces perseverance. Perseverance will refine our character, and proven character leads us back to HOPE. And this hope is not a disappointing fantasy, but the hope that will make us experience the endless love of God cascading into our hearts. This hope will help us understand that in our nothingness, we experience MORE of God... the fullness and richness of HIS LOVE.

Life is all about experiencing God in every season. The ultimate purpose of living is intimacy with God.

To see Him, to hear Him, to taste and see that He is good! He doesn't want His children to suffer because He is a good Father who gives good gifts, whose yoke is easy and whose burden is light. He wants us to know that in our suffering, He is there to be our oasis. He is there to give us refreshment and rest.

He is there and He will never leave. In our suffering, He teaches us to see things beyond what our naked and myopic human eyes can see. He wants us to see things the way He does.

In our deepest pain and fear; in our ugliest, loneliest and darkest moments; in our brokenness, stubbornness, nothingness, helplessness and hopelessness, we remain as the apple of His eyes.

In Him,

we are forgiven and accepted

we are worthy and made holy

we are enough.

we are rich and never in lack

we are beautiful and loved.

We can trust Him even in the valley of the shadow of death. The comfort of His love takes away all fears. We will never walk alone, for He is close to the poor and the brokenhearted. His authority is our strength and peace. He remains the Sovereign God and loving Father who will never get tired of telling us HOW PRECIOUS we are to Him.

"we also glory in tribulations, knowing that tribulation produces perseverance; and perseverance, character; and character, hope. Now hope does not disappoint, because the love of God

has been poured out in our hearts by the Holy Spirit who was given to us."

Romans 5:3-5

Has life been cruel?

This year may have been hurtful and challenging to some of us. Some were diagnosed with cancer, COVID or an incurable disease. Some were abandoned by their husband or wife. Some were abused. Some suddenly lost a father, a loving mother or a child. Some lost their jobs and some declared bankruptcy.

You may have experienced being homeless. You discovered that your husband is having an affair, or your child is addicted to drugs. You had a broken family and been through broken relationships. You were sued and lost the case. Your character was maligned, and you were bullied. You had a serious fight with your brother, sister or your closest friend. Your parents hated you and cursed you. You were depressed and almost gave up on life. Bad news never stopped coming. You felt alone and prayers were left UNANSWERED.

And when you think of the past year, you only see pain, sorrow, grief, chaos, darkness, turmoil and hopelessness.

When people around you are celebrating for new seasons, here you are, having a hard time to see the beauty in your circumstances. You are afraid, anxious and anhedonic to move forward.

But you know what,

GOD's GLORY IS IN THE NEWNESS OF THINGS.

Look at you now, despite everything that happened in the past year, you finished the year STRONG. You are still standing and fighting a good fight of faith. You may have not noticed it but the struggles you have been through did not destroy you, instead, it strengthened you, taught you meaningful lessons and caused you to grow in faith.

Somebody said, when driving a car, there is a reason why the wind shield is bigger than the side mirrors. It is because you are meant to focus on looking forward and just take a glance on the past once in a while. We are not meant to get stuck in the past. We are all meant to move forward!

Take your time to grieve if you lost someone or something, but never forget to MOVE FORWARD, little by little, day after day. Do not just lie down, RISE UP! God is the God of the future. He is already there. He is preparing a BRAND-NEW thing for you this year. Receive it. Embrace it.

Know that even in your most uncertain time, you are secured in His hands. Even when no human help is available, He remains to be faithful. Through the storm, He is your firm foundation. In the midst of this ever-changing, fast-pacing world, you can find rest in His presence.

There is nothing you have lost that He can't replace.

He is the Father to the fatherless and the Lover of your soul. He gives peace and provision.

None of His promises ever failed. He orchestrates your life for your good. He is everything that your soul could ever long for.

His strength is made perfect in your weaknesses. He will help you start all over again. He listens, sees and cares about you. He can take your darkest night and turn it to shining light.

***For I'm going to do a brand-new thing. See, I have already begun! Don't you see it? I will make a road through the wilderness of the world for my people to go home, and create rivers for them in the desert!
Isaiah 43:19***

Should I thank God for delays?

Yes, the same way that you should thank Him for closed doors, wrecked plans, denied applications, detours, 'rejections', and heart breaks. Thank him for seasons of waiting and quarantine.

People often sees a delay as God's punishment. But a delay doesn't mean God's denial. Sometimes, a delay means a signal to pause, pray, fast and inquire of God. It is God prompting you to

drop all your plans,

prepare your blank notepad,

carefully listen to His instructions and

log His plans on your 'to-do' list.

Pushing your plans too hard may extend your tour to your self-made wilderness. You test your plan A, then

Plan B, C, D…Z without the clarity of what God wants, is a dangerous risk. You have been too focused on a goal that is not God's. It doesn't mean it's a goal with wrong motive, but maybe, a goal that is just unaligned to God's good, pleasing and perfect will.

You ask God, 'what did I do wrong that I should wait this long? Am I that bad that you withhold your favor from me?'. Sometimes, you get sick and tired of His reply, "My child, trust me, I have greater plans". You stop talking to friends who tell you the same. You stop dreaming and hoping. Your delays made your view of God distorted, fogged and hyperopic.

My friend, know that God is a personal God – He is beside you, behind you, before you and within you. He never stopped loving and caring for you. He heard your objections, your rants, your pleas and your valid justifications. He knows your motives, your thoughts and your heart's desire. He knows where exactly your pains are coming from. He fully understands why your soul is downcast. Never think otherwise.

He never stopped being a God… never stopped being your loving ABBA Father whose plans for you are FAULTLESS and FLAWLESS. His timing is perfect, never advance nor delayed. You cannot compare His calendar with your timetable. You can't compare His infinite mind with your finite view of things.

Sarah gave birth past her reproductive years. Hannah was medically sterile when she bore Samuel. Noah built the ark even there were no signs that it will rain hard. The bleeding woman waited for 12 years before she got healed. Jacob waited for the love of his life, Rachel, for 14 long years. Joseph had to wait through many troubles before he received vindication and freedom, see his dreams fulfilled, and reunite with his father.

They waited quite long in human perspective, but in God's view of things, everything happened right on time to reveal and magnify His glory in them. The purpose of your life is beyond ticking items in your bucket list. The very reason why you finished a degree, why you work, excel, get healed, get married, bear children, build a family, prosper in life, go on a mission is solely to make God known and to glorify His name through us. He is preparing something beautiful and praiseworthy for you, He will not settle for less. When the time is right, God will make it happen (Isaiah 60:22)

Don't call it a DELAY.
It's God's PERFECT TIME!

We wait for that which we value. Surely, when the time of reaping has come, you will thank Him for sustaining you in your season of waiting. Know that the fruits of obedience are sweet and satisfying. Build godly character as you wait. Know God more, love Him more and experience Him more.

Trust God completely, He knows what He is doing.

"He makes all things beautiful IN HIS TIME".
Ecclesiastes 3:11

Dream Again

The mountains you are facing and the waves you are trying to overcome are meant to strengthen and hone you to the kind person that God designed you to be. As you go through these challenges, God wants you to trust and depend on Him more.

They are meant to bring out the best, and not the monster in you; to build you, and not to destroy you; to unite you, and not to break you.

You work so hard to fulfill your dreams without knowing that overstretching yourself can sometimes snatch your joy, patience and self-control. In that way, you hurt others, you hurt yourself and hurt God. The enemy can subtly use your busy-ness for you to lose control over the things that matter most.

Make your rest and your time with the Lord, non-negotiable. Your intimacy with God will refresh you and prepare you to fly. Know that God can restore everything that the enemy has stolen from you.

God will restore your joy as you stay with Him. He will build your life as you abide in Him. He will renew your mind. He will fill your heart with love and compassion. He will make you see His mercies that are new every morning. Dream and plan with Him again. Soar with Him and hope in Him again. He will help you reconnect and build godly relationships with your family, friends and workmates.

He will make you experience the life that only Jesus can give, a life in its fullest measure.

"The thief's purpose is to steal, kill and destroy.

My purpose is to give life in all its fullness."

John 10:10

Failure is an open door

If Jabez was born in pain, I almost came into a conclusion that I was born to fail. I had a fair share of tears and pains in high school due to Arts— when a simple 'paper mache' project made me hate myself and thought of quitting school (no exaggeration); ; in college, Zoology 113 (comparative anatomy) made me think I was having Dementia in the young.

But Med school won the race, that fair share blew up into a major share. I cried a river of tears because of series of falling and failing; mental block and exam-induced stupor. I had a bad start in medschool, really bad! Every failed quiz and exam snatched my confidence. I almost believed that Medical School was not for me. I felt small, inferior and humiliated. I felt unworthy, cursed and hopeless.

Those were years of oozing emotional bleed overflowing profusely.

Basag na basag na, durog na durog pa! By God's grace, I just endured and embraced the pain. I allowed God to take care of me and to heal every wound. I held on tightly to His promises and soaked myself into His word.

Little did I know that my failure, my delay and my pain were God's gateway for me to know my purpose and to find my victory as an aspiring doctor.

Had my 'second wind', my 'balikwas' moment, when I was in third year.

I realized that those pains were necessary, not to break me but to enlarge my territory. Rejection was God's protection. A closed door was God's way to lead me to the right perspective, attitude and direction.

The memories of those pains turned into 'AHA! moments'. I never knew I would be dealing with people (patients and students) who are going through a similar roadblock as I had before. God used my stories to encourage them and show them that hope is real.

Every time I see my patients, I vividly remember how I walked aimlessly in university grounds thinking that being a doctor is an impossible dream and that I was just fighting in vain. Truly, God's ways and thoughts are higher than ours. Thank God He embraced me on those million times that I was at the verge of giving up Med School. No wonder the palpable desire to become a doctor never left my heart and my prayers.

I read this poem decades ago (credits to the author), I hope it will encourage you as much as it did to me:

Failure doesn't mean you're a failure,
it does mean God's timing is different from yours.

Failure doesn't mean you haven't accomplished something,
it does mean He wants you to learn what really matters in life.

Failure doesn't mean you've been a fool,
it does mean you have a lot of faith.

Failure doesn't mean you've been disgraced,
it does mean you are made stronger for the battle

Failure doesn't mean you don't have it,
it does mean you have to do something in a different way.

Failure doesn't mean you're inferior,
it does mean you're not perfect.

Failure doesn't mean you've wasted your time,
it does mean you have a reason to start fresh.

Failure doesn't mean you should give up,

it does mean you should get up and continue a walk of faith.

Failure doesn't mean you'll never make it,
it does mean He wants you to experience Him as you wait.

Failure doesn't mean God has abandoned you,
it does mean HE IS JUST FIXING YOU.

The God of our waiting time

I don't know about you, but for me, waiting is tough! I used to hate waiting. Why is waiting so hard? Because waiting implies that we do not have control over circumstances in our lives. Our nature is to plan our future. We want to control when to finish college, when to get married and have children, when to get promoted, when to buy properties and when to retire. We think that we own our destiny, yet we can honestly admit that we can barely see beyond today.

We live and work day by day but sometimes those days seem to drag out. Waiting is the time and season in our lives that can become unbearable if we lose sight of what really matters.

In Psalm 27, David was expressing angst over the adversaries in his life but he also freely expressed the deep cry of his heart. It is a cry that is centered on his utmost desire to simply be with God... to stay and gaze on Him like watchmen wait for the dawn, more than anything.

DAVID WANTED TO SIMPLY BE WITH THE LORD.

Sometimes, while we are waiting, we are too focused on when the blessing or the answer will finally arrive. We often overlook the BEST part of waiting... and that is EXPERIENCING GOD.

When our eyes are fixed on HIM, we can spend the whole day and night marveling in the Lord's perfection, gazing upon His beauty, seeking Him in His Temple, listening to His instructions, worshipping Him with shouts of joy, praising Him with the melodies of our hearts, dancing with Him and enjoying His presence.

This gives our 'waiting time' a new meaning.

It is no longer burdensome or agonizing.

It turned into a time to learn and grow; a time to cultivate relationship with him.

Success, abundance, health, loved ones or any earthly thing can never satisfy. Only God does.

Like David, the ONE THING I ask of the Lord through all the seasons of my life is to dwell in His house NOW AND FOREVER.

Need a Miracle?

I took Biology, then Medicine then Molecular Biology and Biotechnology. We studied a lot about evolution, genetic engineering, physics, chemistry and drugs. We studied the physiology of life and death.

But to date, science still failed to fully define and explain MIRACLES.

One of my favorite accounts in the bible is the story of Elijah during the contest on Mount Carmel in 1 Kings 18. Read it and see for yourselves how God moved in miraculous ways. Elijah was courageous because he knew how powerful and mighty his God is. He boldly asked his God for a MIRACLE. He asked for a supernatural thing to happen to show his enemies that his God is the One true God.

He asked God to FLASH DOWN FIRE from heaven. How can that be possible? It is not even natural for fire to fall from the skies, right? Some says that fire meant 'lightning', but even so, how can lightning occur without a thundercloud? Remember, it hasn't been raining for 3 years that time!

But after Elijah prayed, He got His miracle immediately! The fire of the Lord flashed down from heaven and burned up the young bull, the wood, the stones, the dust including all the water in the trench. Everything was consumed! This astonished everyone who saw it, they fell face down on the ground and cried, "the Lord, he is God! Yes, the Lord is God!".

Whatever miracle you are praying for, remember and believe that GOD IS ABLE. No matter what science tells you, no matter what the doctors say, no matter how the enemy is convincing you to doubt God, be confident that if we ask anything according to His will, it will be given to you! God makes all things possible.

God heals. He can burn up all lesions in your body and bring back your strength!

He provides. If He can provide fire from heaven, how can He not provide for all your needs?

He restores health and relationships.

He hears your cry and honors the desires of your heart.

He is victorious.

Believe God and you will see.

"This is the confidence we have in approaching God: that if we ask anything according to his will, he hears us. And if we know that he hears us—whatever we ask—we know that we have what we asked of him."

1 John 5:14-15

God provides

"God's work done in God's way will never lack in supply". This quote by James Hudson Taylor has been one of my favorites through the years. The 'work of God' is not limited in the church or in the mission field. This work also refers to His great work in your family, your loved ones and YOUR LIFE.

If you are in great need, but your CAPACITY to earn makes it hard for you to raise funds, remember the story of the widow who cried out to Elisha. She only had a jar of oil. Elisha instructed the widow to collect empty jars without telling her the reason why. Elisha was sure of one thing, God will provide. True enough, the Lord miraculously multiplied the oil over and over to its unthinkable abundance.

God knows that your funds are low. He knows that you can only produce 'this much'. Believe that God can fill every empty jar that you lay down before Him. When the son told his mother the good problem that there is no more jar, I am guessing that her self-talk was, "I should have collected more jars!"

Believe that God will never let you go hungry, begging for bread. He will not leave you empty handed. He will never abandon His children. He is a good Father. He is the source of everything! Elisha told them, "Now sell the olive oil and pay your debts, and you and your sons can live on what is left over."

The way to go is not to apply for loans or chase for people to borrow money from, but to come to God to ask for wisdom and provision. Plan with Him, work with Him and allow Him to amaze you with His wonderful plans for your life. He longs to provide for you generously.

Trust him that he can provide all your needs according to His riches in glory through Christ, no matter how impossible it is. Know that, nothing is too difficult for Him.

"By God's mighty power at work within us is able to do far more than we would ever dare to ask or even dream of—infinitely beyond our highest prayers, desires, thoughts, or hopes."

Ephesians 3: 20

Healing

Doctors also need a Healer

We live in an imperfect world. Medicine is an imperfect science.

We are in crisis not only financially, but also culturally, morally and in identity. We face troubles. We get confused with our emotions. We want more but achieve less. Our minds are full of whys. We get frustrated with ourselves. There are inevitable circumstances that are out of our control.

Doctors also need healing. Engineers are also people under construction. Dentists also need 'filling' for strength and restoration. Pilots need someone to control their flights. Tour guides need direction and navigation. Counselors also need comfort and counselling. Computer programmers need to abide with the codes created by their Master Programmer to solve life's problems. Teachers need instruction and mentoring. An author also needs someone to write his seasons and chapters. Architects need to go back to his original design in order to function efficiently.

Nurses need caring. Mothers need nurturing. Fathers need a Father's love.

No matter how far we have gone through, despite our position and titles.

We fail. We struggle. We need help. We need fixing. We need healing.

We are all 'sick' in many different aspects. Jesus came for the sick, not for the healthy. But we need to acknowledge that we need healing before we get healed. The Greatest Physician can heal and restore you physically, mentally, emotionally and spiritually. He can renew your strength and make you soar like an eagle. He can mend your broken dreams. He can fix your broken relationship with your loved ones and with Him.

He knows your thoughts, He sees your tears, He hears your cry for help. He can be trusted. He knows you are struggling. He knows your fears. He is ready to restore and heal you. All you need do is to come as you are. Don't be afraid. He can be trusted because His love for you is unconditional, gentle and kind. He wants you to be free from your 'sickness'.

He is the God who can save you from your current situation. He is a mighty Savior. He can save you from the threats of your past, present and future. He is just a prayer away. Seek Him and You will find Him.

"You will seek me and find me when you seek me with all your heart.

I will be found by you," declares the LORD. JEREMIAH 29:13

Touch His robe

Since I was in Medical School, I always had attachment with cancer patients. It grew stronger when my very own mother had Colon Cancer. If you are a cancer patient, this is for you.

I understand that your journey may be frustrating at times. You have done everything over the years, consulted many doctors and spent everything you had for treatments. But the cancer is still there, to some, it even got worse. Until now, you are hoping and waiting for the doctor to tell you that you are completely healed.

I remember the bleeding woman in the bible. She has the same situation. She heard about Jesus, she came behind Him through the crowd and TOUCHED His robe. In her heart, she knew that if she will touch His robe, she will be healed. Miraculously, the bleeding stopped immediately. When Jesus saw her, He said, "your FAITH has made you well. Your suffering is over." What a relief!

Declaring that your suffering will be over very soon. It's not the act of touching the robe that healed her, but the FAITH that Jesus can heal her completely. Her faith brought her healing and freedom.

God is aware of the utmost desires of your heart. Don't think otherwise. Even if things seem to get worse, hold on to the truth that God is bigger than all the troubles in the world. In Him healing is POSSIBLE. He goes beyond what the doctors and science tell you. You are healed by Christ's finished work at the cross of Calvary. He has won over all sickness, sin, poverty and death.

I speak life, good health, peace, abundance, joy and grace to you. May you continue to find courage and hope in the Lord. Keep the faith. Keep the faith.

"Take heart, daughter," he said, "your faith has healed you."

And the woman was healed at that moment."
Matthew 9:22

Healing or Healer?

When the 10 lepers met Jesus, they asked for mercy, not even for 'healing'. Their desire is not just for the skin lesions to dry and clear up but also for mercy to experience Jesus and be free from the stigma and the hurts of 'outcasts' like them. Jesus did not tell them they were healed and there was no instant healing, instead, Jesus instructed them to show themselves to the priest. It's like an assurance of healing because during those times, only the priests can validate when the patient is cured from leprosy. These 10 men followed Jesus' instructions even without the visible evidence of healing. They believed, they were already healed.

On their way to the priest, they we're amazed to see that their lesions completely disappeared. They were clean and there was no evidence of active disease. They were bursting with joy, of course! But when one of them saw he was healed, he came back to Jesus to praise Him and thank Him. He threw himself at Jesus' feet and worshipped Him. Nine lepers had faith and enjoyed the blessing but didn't bother to give thanks to Jesus because they were after the blessing of healing. Only one had faith and was after experiencing the power and the presence of the Healer. The rest was too focused on the provision, while this one man chased and sought after the Provider. That one man didn't just give thanks but fell faced down to worship and give glory to Jesus. He knew that the miracle was from Jesus. His only hope was Jesus.

Sometimes in life, healing comes after we experienced a change of heart and a change of focus. The moment that our eyes are already fixed solely on Jesus is also the time that we receive the blessing of real healing.

Few weeks before my mother left us, she said she wants to be discharged from the hospital and stay home with family. As a doctor, I was trying to convince her to comply with treatments. But she told me she had peace when God gave her Psalms 23. She wanted to spend time worshipping God at home, with family. She was confident about her decision. We felt her joy and peace when we brought her home; she kept on embracing and kissing us ; whenever friends visit her, she would spend time worshipping God with them. She wasn't even struggling on her last days. Lo and behold, the whole family including her close friends were singing and worshipping God together until that final hour that she went home to Jesus.

Healing for her is experiencing Jesus.

Will you dare to believe that you are healed even without any evidence of healing? Will you praise God even before receiving the blessing? Do you go back to God to worship Him for every answered prayer? Do you take time to thank Him for the blessings you didn't even ask for?

Do you long for healing or the Healer?

"You're all I want in heaven! You're all I want on earth!
I'm in the very presence of God— oh, how refreshing it is!
I've made Lord GOD my home.

God, I'm telling the world what you do!" Psalm 73: 25-28

Behind the mask

Few years ago, the 'BIG ONE' caused fear especially in Luzon as it was projected to be a 'very destructive' intensity 8 earthquake. Fear also surrounded CALABARZON and NCR when Taal Volcano erupted last year because of the warning that another 'hazardous' explosive eruption is very possible within hours. The bush fire triggered fear in Australia, flash flood happened in Indonesia, heavy snow in Pakistan and locust plague in Africa. We experienced, Typhoons Rolly, Siony, Tonyo and Ulysses. And of course, the so-called major world changer, CORONAVIRUS global pandemic happened last year.

In all these natural and inevitable calamities, none of them ever defeated mankind. Not because we are strong, because in contrary, we are fearful individuals who do not have the capability to control catastrophe. We overcome because we know that the most effective strategy is to keep the faith. We surrender everything to the One who controls everything.

The crisis is real. But God is above all your realities. He can steady your heart amidst the crisis. You stand strong because your confidence is in your Sovereign God. He holds all things together. He holds your world in His hands. Hold on to your faith despite all legitimate and valid reasons to fear because your battle is God's battle.

You've been hard pressed on every side, but not crashed; perplexed but not driven to despair; hunted down, but never abandoned by God. Whatever situation you are in right now, COVID-related or not, never believe the lie that God is far away. He is not just watching mankind from a distance. He is with you.

Masks, gloves, PPEs, disinfectants and vaccines can protect us. But God is our ultimate protection.

Detection kits and laboratory tests can identify some illness, but we can only trust the omniscient God who knows everything. Medicines and supplements can give remedy, but only our all-powerful God can restore you to complete health.

Beyond the world's quest to find the cure for COVID, God remains the only solution.

It is unfair to say that these doctors and nurses who passed away 'SUCCUMBED' to coronavirus, because this is not a lost battle. Healing is as possible as the blue skies, the clean air, clear waters and empty roads that we saw in Metro Manila during the lockdown. It was just a wishful thinking, but it happened! Faith sees the invisible, believes the unbelievable and receives the impossible. We do not yield to bad news, we do not submit to coronavirus, we do not concede to the disease, we do not bow down to death. All those were already defeated by the blood of Jesus when He died on the cross of Calvary for our sins to manifest His sacrificial and beautiful love. We only bow down and surrender to the ONLY SOLUTION to all these: our ultimate, greatest and most Sovereign God who embraces us with His unconditional love.

"Great is our Lord and mighty in power;
his understanding has no limit."
Psalm 147:4-5

I love you, Doc

I was praying for a patient one day. It was a prayer of thanksgiving and declaration of healing. The patient was fervently praying with me and when I said 'In Jesus Name, AMEN'. He said 'AMEN' and shouted 'I LOVE YOU DOC JAZZ' in tears.

And I responded, 'Thank You for showing such strong faith that inspired me to be strong as well (in my own battles)'. How I wish I was able to video or capture that moment. This patient was discriminated by his family and the society. He had a terminal illness, he was alone and afraid. But he was in faith that he will be healed and will reconcile with family. He said it was the first time that someone prayed for him.

It's always humbling to receive these words from people I work for (patients, students and coworkers), always amazed how they acknowledge the power of God to turn their situations around. Aside from that, I am thankful that God is creating friendship and building faith from simple seeds of compassion.

I cannot trade this profession for riches. I see miracles in my patients' lives, I get chances to pray for them and comfort them. Some of them even made a great impact in my life that made them 'mainstays' in my life testimony.

Kristine had leukemia. She had one son. I was walking in Ward 3 at around 4am, when I saw her waving her hand. I approached her and she hugged me so tight. No words, she was just in tears. I comforted her and told her to sleep. Then I went home after my duty (8am). The next day, I learned that she passed away few hours after I left the hospital.

Kim had germinoma in the brain. He was 11 years old but walks like a stroke patient because of the tumor. One day, her mom called me and asked me to pray for Kim because he cannot breathe. I went to their home and prayed for him. He recovered. Miraculously, He was able to walk and go back to school. He was able to do his therapy as well in a wellness gym.

Nanay Siling was our neighbor with cancer of the tongue. I saw her with disposable napkin on her chin. I asked what that was for. She said, she's in pain, the tumor was bleeding, and she cannot go to the hospital. I was still a student then. All I can afford was 20 pieces of Mefenamic Acid hoping that it could give some relief. Thank God the pain was gone. The next day, she gave me a *Kerokerokeropi* stuffed toy. I said she should have bought medicines from her money. But she insisted to give it to me as her gift gratitude for making her realize that her life was still worth fighting for.

Baby JP was a newborn baby boy with imperforated anus. He was left by his mom in the emergency room. The pediatric resident and I took care of him and raised funds for his operation. The operation was successful. I was praying to adopt him. But few days after his operation, that was Christmas Day 2006, I was already in a different department, the nurses told me that he died of hypothermia. It was painful, because I was already preparing myself to call him 'my son'.

Thank God for the privilege to be a blessing. Be God's His hands and feet for the 'least', the 'lost' and the 'last'. God molds our character as we serve people who can't give back. Max Lucado once said, ***"I will be kind... for such is how God has treated me."***

The stories of friendship I mentioned above are not reflections of my own kindness, but of God's. It's not about my strength, but His grace that is perfect in my weaknesses. It's not about my love, but His great love that covered all my mess, sins and shame.

When he saw the crowds, he had compassion on them, because they were harassed and helpless, like sheep without a shepherd.

Matthew 9:36

Broken to whole

I was 13 years old and depressed. I looked at the mirror and saw a hopeless, hated, ugly and emotionally tortured young girl. I was sick and tired of all the blame and shame. I did something wrong, but I was confused why my punishment, though not physical, hits the very core of my heart and broke it into pieces. Do I deserve this? I said.

But that stare at the mirror that night brought me to my knees. I sought the ONE who said I am fearfully and wonderfully made. I surrendered my life to Him and accepted Him as my Lord and Savior. Since then, I started to experience the love that keeps no record of wrongs!

It brought so much change in me. I got so excited to live because I already knew the purpose why I live. I had fervor in academics because I was so sure of the reasons I need to learn. I never get tired of sharing that testimony to my friends and classmates.

But life wasn't perfect. We are not exempted from challenges because we still live in a troubled world. Along the way, thereafter, especially as an adult, I had my share of failures, heartbreaks, losses, relational blues, pains, emotional chaos, fears, insecurities, pride, threats, rejections, bad decisions, bad reactions and bad thoughts. Name it, I had it! I went through several seasons that made me see life and myself ugly and worthless again.

But the Savior who took me from the miry clay consistently rushed to catch me. He stubbornly embraced me with the same love He gave that night that I surrendered my life to Him. Constantly, I found myself amazed how this God of the heavens relentlessly pursues a person like me. Who am I to deserve this?

I am not deserving, and I am not entitled of any blessing, but God chose to love and stay. He never left my side. He never forgets. HE HAS ALWAYS BEEN THERE.

He taught my eyes to see the BEAUTY in pain, hardships and death. He kissed every tear and healed every wound. God walked with me through the rain and taught me how to dance with it! He gathered all the fragments of my heart so that no part of me is apart from Him!

27 years later, as I stare at the mirror again today, I see a product of God's amazing grace. I smile differently because I see differently. I no longer see my job as a heavy burden, but an avenue to work based on the analogy of God's work in creating the world. I no longer see my beauty based on human standards but on God's benchmark. He has carefully woven every part of me from nothing to something, His workmanship is marvelous, how can I not be beautiful? I no longer see my worth based on who rejected me in the past, but on the high price JESUS paid to redeem me. He purchased me with His own blood!

"What can make me whole again?
Nothing but the blood of Jesus!"

Cancer Patients

Remembering all cancer patients in prayer today.

All eyes are focused on our current health crisis and the pandemic. But we have friends who braved going to the hospital to undergo surgery, chemotherapy and radiation therapy. Some needed to stay in the hospital despite the fear of being infected because they badly need IV medications.

If you are this person, I prayed for you. A lot of people are praying for you. God is using your doctors, your medications, your food, your family and your friends to make you well and to heal you. He is filling your heart with faith, gladness, hope and courage because His name is glorified through your story.

Declaring peace that exceeds human understanding. The lover of your soul, Jesus, holds your heart. He is watching over you. Praying that hope will arise in your heart as you continually fix your eyes on Jesus. By His wounds you have been healed. His finished work on the cross nailed and defeated all kinds of sickness. It conquered death.

God knows your utmost desire to be completely healed. God hears you. He cares for you. There might be some bad news along the way but 'GREATER IS HE' that is living in you, than all the troubles around you. Nothing is too difficult for Him. Impossible things are His specialty. Surrender your health and your life to Jesus. He is trustworthy. He alone SAVES. You can be confident and fearless because You know in Christ, victory is sure.

My Mom faced cancer with joy and faith. We always pray together. Her joy comes from the assurance that her God is her Savior and His faithfulness is as sure as the morning. It was 17 months of battle but she didn't suffer hair loss, no major complications from surgery and chemotherapy, didn't severely lost appetite. There was no significant 'weight loss' until her last 2 weeks. God faithfully provided for all her medical expenses. No one noticed she had cancer unless she would tell it. She fought her battle praying and expressing her faith to every single person she met. She kept her joy, she has always been a source of encouragement, she forgave those who offended her, she trusted the Lord fully.

It was 17 months of roller coaster of emotions, but God took care of every worry and doubt. It was 17 months of stories of healing, miracles, answered prayers and indescribable peace. We may have lost her, but we didn't lose the battle. We definitely won the victory! In Christ, she is completely healed. God was glorified!

I had a patient who has the same case as my mom, Colon Cancer Stage 4. God has a different story for her. She has been a survivor for 7 years now and living a healthy and stress-free life in Australia. God restored her health and has been inspiring other cancer patients.

I had a student who had lung cancer when He was 18. His mom died of cancer. But he was healed. Guess what, He finished Medicine and is now a licensed doctor. His story inspired a lot of sick children aspiring to become successful professionals in the future.

Whatever story you have, God be glorified in your testimony, my friend. Face cancer with faith. Count your blessings and thank God for everything. Keep the faith, it's worth it! Pray and encourage someone who has cancer today.

"By His stripes we are healed". Isaiah 53:5

He puts all shackles off my feet

My father taught me the basics of Karate when I was 7. My cousins learned about it. They tried to test my skills by tying my hands and feet and challenged me to release myself. I didn't know how to apply Karate in that situation, I tried, but futile. I ended up crying, screaming to ask help from my grandpa. Fast forward in grade school, when my father learned that my sister and I fought and hurt each other, he dragged us to the second floor, tied our feet with rope (and ants) and hanged us (semi) upside down. We were prideful at first and still fighting with words. But my Dad told us that he will not remove the rope until we reconcile. We had no choice but to ask forgiveness and embrace each other.

Some shackles are not metal nor ropes. Some are anger, brokenness, unforgiveness, malice, fornication, hurtful words, insecurity, lies, emptiness and loneliness. We may try to be free from them, but efforts are futile. We need supernatural power and strength to be completely free. But that power doesn't come from us. Only Jesus can totally free us from the power of sin, shame and death.

When Jesus came into my life, the change was gradual. Little by little, as the Lord was revealing me the truth about my identity and His great love, every shackle was slowly released.

His pure, unconditional, indescribable and unfathomable love changed my story. Apart from Him, I am a nobody, I can do no good thing and I can do nothing. But with Him, no matter what people say and no matter how dark the valleys may appear to be, I WILL NOT FEAR because God is my victory.

"If you abide in my word, you are truly my disciples,

and you will know the truth, and the truth will set you free"

(John 8:31-32)

Relationships

Imperfect parents

We all have our share of misunderstandings with our parents. We don't like their way of disciplining us, we get pissed when our moms nag in the morning or when they ask us to wash the dishes. We take it (seriously) against them when they miss to attend our competitions and recognition days. We often argue about clothes, food, course, job, relationships, clash of personalities, decisions and choices in life.

But no matter what kind of parenting they raised us with, one truth remains: it is God who appointed them to be our parents and we are commanded to honor, obey, respect and love them.

It is a great privilege to serve our imperfect parents.

It's a privilege to take their unsolicited advice often misinterpreted as 'pakielamera advise', to know their thoughts on our issues in life, to listen to their morning 'litanya', to read their text messages asking

"San na u?" and hear their honest and sometimes hurtful comments about our grammar, clothes, make up, weight, grades and attitude.

It is a privilege to treat them on special occasions and even on ordinary days. It's a great pleasure to stay with them and take care of them realizing that after all these years, our time with them is far more valuable than our time to fulfill our dreams and travel around the world.

It is a privilege to hear them call us, "Anak..."

When my Mama was on her sick bed, I found the greatest honor in changing her diaper, feeding her, giving her medicines, bathing her and nursing her when she had discomforts. I realized it was more honorable than receiving medals and professional degrees.

It's a privilege to understand their tantrums, to bless, listen, comfort and pray for them. What an honor to respect and love them despite their imperfections. God appointed them to be our parents. Whether we think they did a great job or not, we are called to honor them as people CHOSEN by God to be their children.

My parents prayed and fought to keep a complete

family for 39 years. They risked and gave up a lot of things to raise us well. No matter how stubborn, unlovable and unworthy we are as children, they still chose to love us, fight for us and pray for us. I will never trade them for silver, gold or any other parents in the world. I take pleasure being their daughter. I love them so much.

Children, obey your parents in the Lord, for this is right. "Honor your father and mother"—which is the first commandment with a promise — "so that it may go well with you and that you may enjoy long life on the earth." Ephesians 6:1-2

Lets Talk

Now that there is no face to face meet ups. We only communicate via messaging apps. Here are some tips for effective communication which I also shared with my students in Medical Practice 2.

1. Learn to reply all the time

It's an act of respect and courtesy to acknowledge what the other person just said. Don't be that person's reason to feel rejected or insecure. Always aim for an edifying ending. If you don't want a lengthy discussion, then end the conversation by at least saying, 'thank you' or clicking any emoticon. Those are forms of polite replies.

2. It won't hurt to express

Kind Expression is a form of vulnerability, humility and honesty. I understand that sometimes you need to be guarded. That's fine. Maybe you had frustrations in the past. Perhaps you were misinterpreted, misquoted or misunderstood. Or maybe, your words were taken for granted. But know that not everyone has the purpose of opposing you. Some are just too willing to risk to befriend, listen, bring out the best in you and share lives with you with no strings attached. 'Stiffness' is understandable but is sometimes harsh. Be a little kinder next time.

3. Don't make a big deal out of small deals

Never assume the person's emotion when you are just reading his comments and replies. Some people aren't too expressive in writing. They mean no harm. When in doubt, ask to confirm. Don't assume. Don't judge. In other words, don't complicate things. On the other hand, don't get intimidated by people who are 'loud' in written communication. Maybe they are loud because they need to be 'heard'. If you can't keep up, don't just leave them behind, refer them to people who can.

4. Speak Life

If you have something good to say, SAY IT! That might be the ONLY word that person has been waiting for to finally believe in HOPE. Reserve your corrective statements after you've neutralized your emotion, calmed down, carefully thought about your concern and picked up constructive words to structure your statement into a wise and loving piece of advice. Release kind words!

5. Aim for Clarity

We were raised differently with different beliefs and cultures. Your message shouldn't just be clear to you. It should be clearer to the receiver. Again, don't assume that "it's understandable" or "it's self-explanatory". Empathize and be fair.

Men are born for relationships. We were made to connect and communicate. Let us honor God through it. Remember,

Kung may nagbibigay, dapat may tatanggap. Isipin mo nag-abot ka ng napakagandang vase tapos walang tumanggap. Diba mahuhulog at mababasag? Sayang. Kung may nagtatanong, dapat may sasagot. Pag nagsasalita ka ng walang kausap, anong tawag sayo? Kung may magmamahal, dapat may tatanggap ng pagmamahal. Pag walang ganon, ang tawag dun, malabo ang usapan!

Relationship is a two-way street, regardless of the level. Whether it's shallow or deep, we don't BREAK relationships, we build it! Right? Don't push people away. Unless your safety and sanity are at risk, draw them closer so you can share the love of Jesus to them. You need wisdom in choosing whom you will allow to enter your life. Keep that caution. But don't forget that the people you meet are sent and handpicked by God for a purpose. You learn and grow through them. Be a light in other's path. Connect to them intentionally. Communicate with them effectively. Create an impact in your community.

"Let us therefore make every effort to do what leads to peace and to mutual edification".
Romans 14:19

Emotional Distancing

Social distancing limits us from public interactions. Hugging, tapping someone's back, high five, social gatherings, face to face meetings are discouraged during the pandemic. But physical distancing may lead us to become impersonal, hostile, isolated, dissociated, apathetic and indifferent. It shortens our conversations to purely transactional. We hold meetings, classes, conferences, birthdays and all other events through several useful platforms…zoom, messenger room, google meet, MS Teams. We are blessed to have them during this time of crisis. But the truth is, nothing beats face-to-face interactions with people, right? It is still best to build and grow relationships with physical interaction.

Unfortunately, we cannot do that during a pandemic.

That is why we are ought to adapt to the call of the times. If we are not cautious, physical distancing could result to a more dangerous side effect. And it's called, emotional distancing. Remember, we are not just in a health crisis. Like domino effect, we are also in a financial, relational and emotional crisis.

If we can strain eyeballs and spend hours working, watching Netflix or doing gaming stuff, I am sure it won't hurt to drop our swords for a while to check how our loved ones are coping. In this season that we are taking all possible measures to save ourselves from acquiring the disease, let us also save one another from loneliness, apathy, callousness and insensitivity.

More than a time for self-care, this is also a time for community care. Apply wisdom at all times. Refuse to be isolated. Avoid conflicts and overlook offenses as much as you can. Be more understanding and caring. Everyone is fighting a battle we know nothing about.

Friends, this is the time to be more intentional. Let the people you care about know that you really care. Let them know that you love, and you are willing to listen. Be that someone who sparks light and hope in this trying time. Remain connected. Talk to people. Express love. Vent out gratitude. Craft uplifting words. Declare blessing. Speak life. Be vocal and appreciate acts of kindness. Let them feel that your relationship is still solid and intact. Teach them to dwell on things that are true, noble, right, pure, lovely, admirable, excellent and praiseworthy. It takes grace and effort to build and maintain relationships.

Do everything to encourage one another.

"May the God who gives endurance and encouragement give you the same

attitude of mind toward each other that Christ Jesus had." Romans 15:5

Status: In a relationship (for 27 years)

Twenty-seven years ago, I was 13. But not the typical 13 years old who was enjoying teenage life. I was not thinking about what to wear, which movie to watch, brand of shoes/clothes, sports, weekend getaways, barkada, fashion, notebook design, kikay kit and crushes. Because I was a tired and exhausted youth.

I was trying to prove something to my family, my school, my friends and to myself. I was trying to erase a bad image brought about by that one wrong decision to cheat in one of my school projects. Consequences were too heavy for me to carry. All the chaos made my heart feel so empty.

January 27, 1994, I was staring at the mirror and saw JAZZIE at her ugliest, loneliest, saddest, darkest, messiest, most helpless and most hopeless state, wanting to sleep and never to wake up again.

But Someone came to offer an intimate, unfailing, irrevocable and eternal relationship with me. The Man who died on the cross to save me and bought me at THE HIGHEST COST, His name is JESUS.

My Jesus caught me when I was falling. He lifted me back into my feet as if He heard my groaning. He rushed to set me free. I accepted HIS offer of love, salvation and eternal life. Since then, He became my Lord, my Savior, my Redeemer and King, my reason for living. Through the years, His love remained the greatest. It never failed. It's constant and unconditional. It remained faithful. It never left me.

But my love for HIM, it failed a million times. I fail Him every day. I had my ups and downs. There were times that I still feel empty, discouraged and doubtful of Him. There was a season that I was too disobedient to the Savior who redeemed me from the miry clay. I wasn't a good steward of my blessings, I was blinded and got hooked with ungodly friendships, I became stubborn, arrogant and self-serving. I did things that I knew will dishonor Him.

But just the same, JESUS stubbornly and consistently sought me and gave me undeserved forgiveness, and grace that He showed me when we first committed to be IN A RELATIONSHIP.

He overwhelmed me with His deeply intimate, far reaching, enduring, endless, extravagant and overflowing love, as if I was too faithful to Him. His love never rejected me. It never condemned nor ignored me. I was never "seen zoned" or "friendzoned". There were no confusing signals, no cold treatments and no record of wrongs. He always chooses me and chases after me. His love teaches and builds. His love is incredibly patient, satisfying and healing. His love is always enough, lacking nothing. His perfect love made me feel secured and significant. I am complete in Him. I stand in awe of that He is and all that He has done. I seek no greater honor than just to know, obey and love Him more.

I was NEVER SINGLE for 27 years. Because my relationship with my Jesus never allowed me to walk through life alone. This is a love story that will last beyond lifetime.

"And I pray that you and all God's holy people will have the power to understand the greatness of Christ's love—how wide and how long and how high and how deep that love is."
Ephesians 3:18

Motivated by love

A lot of doors opened this year. Doors that I never even prayed for. My routine, vision and dreams changed; my words, my friends and my prayers also suddenly CHANGED.

From an introvert person with a myopic vision. My students and my patients suddenly became the apple(s) of my eyes.

Many are asking about my intentions. They asked,
"Why do you do that?",
"Why do you exert for an extra mile?"
"Aren't you just wasting your time?"
"why do you give them time?"

Honestly, I don't know how to put accurate answers into words. It's beyond description. We do a common thing in an uncommon manner because that is exactly what God is telling us to do. What separates extra milers from the others is the drive to do more than what is expected or required. This EXTRA MILE is motivated by the love of Christ.

When we speak life to students, we don't just talk to them as if they are our subordinates. We hone them as Jesus would. We talk to them as generation builders and as people who will see things differently. We bring out the leader in them and we help develop their inner strength, their character, courage and faith as future leader of nations. We raise them as world changers!

When we treat patients, we don't just diagnose and prescribe. We give them the best quality service and we care for them as Jesus would: we spend time to understand their pains, doubts and fears. We address their apprehensions and encourage them with the truth that God can heal.

In one of our company's National Conferences, I was asked to close in prayer. I planned to just close in prayer! But God had other plans. He led me to pray for our managers who were sick, those who were going through depression and those who were experiencing trials in the family. The Lord also led me to pray for people who served the company selflessly. The session hall was filled with tears while we were praying. Some managers approached me and said that, the closing prayer was the highlight of the whole conference. Some asked for a sort of a 'counselling' and some shared the specific battles they were going through.

It could have been a typical closing prayer, but God wanted it to be done in an uncommon manner. Let us not be discouraged to be 'unconventional'. God allows us to be different so that people may see why we are different. A little more patience, a little more faith, a little more kindness can go a long way. We rise by lifting others. An extra mile unveils someone's genuine smile. No act of kindness is ever wasted.

Kindness may seem to cost nothing but means everything.

And may the Lord make your love to grow and overflow to each other and to everyone else, just as our love does toward you. This will result in your hearts being made strong, sinless, and holy by God our Father so that you may stand before him guiltless on that day when our Lord Jesus Christ returns with all those who belong to Him.

1 Thessalonians 3:12-13

Simple joys

I am on leave today. There's no occasion, I'm not in a vacation, I just want a day off from work. I want to see a new place, meet new students, experience new things. I had concrete plans today.

But God had a better plan. He wanted me to learn SIMPLE JOYS while on leave.

Joy to help. I met people whose greatest joy was to find a patent vein for IV insertion. Everybody rejoiced after a successful search for that precious vein.

Joy to finish strong. I met a courageous woman who managed to bravely finish all medical procedures with grace despite her bruised arms, weak knees and bloated abdomen.

Joy to be recharged. I met students who patiently waited just to be rekindled and recharged from a tiring and exhausting mind work and legwork in Med school.

Joy to be with family. I met children who dropped everything today just to attend to the medical needs of their mother.

Joy to learn. I met medical clerks who refused any merit (24 hour free day) because they don't want to miss any learnings they can get from showing up in the hospital.

Joy to fight. I met a son who was afraid but knew that there were more important things than fear. He knew that His faith in Jesus will deliver them.

Joy to trust. I met a daughter who got the bad result of her mom's laboratory tests. She still joyfully said, "I know God is in control and He already healed my mom."

Joy to love. I met a wife who chose to serve and forgive her husband even though he never said sorry.

Joy to serve. I met a woman who spent the whole day listening, serving and encouraging people around her.

My body was tired but my heart is so full of gratitude to meet these amazing people in one day

"Do not grieve, for the joy of the Lord is your strength." Nehemiah 8:10

He thinks about me

It is comforting, awe-inspiring and enriching to know that Someone is thinking about you. It is a treasure that is worth keeping. Who am I that God is mindful of me? How priceless, how cherished are His thoughts about me, how dear to me is His relentless attention?

I am poor, imperfect and needy and yet, God turned His face on me. He showered me with love though He knew full WELL that I fail every day. My heart is filled with awe to know that the infinite mind of God would turn His attention to a person like me: an insignificant, useless and unworthy trash. He knew me perfectly, but He personally gathered every single broken, ugly and hopeless fragment of me and gave me LIFE in exchange, a life in its fullest measure!

How come the God of the universe, the Darling of heaven, the Prince of Peace, the King of kings would think about a person like me? But it is never an effort for a perfect God and a loving Father do such things for His beloved children. He thought of me even before I was born, He formed all my body parts together in my mother's womb, His eyes were on me when I was going through storms, winds and waves. He thinks of me while I was suffering and in pain. He thought about my health, my success, my fears, my frustrations and anxieties, my dreams and the longings of my heart. He dealt with all of them one by one. He thought about my good, my future, my success, my growth, strength, healing, peace, forgiveness, salvation and eternal life. He thought of giving me a second chance, a third chance, fourth, fifth and many more chances. He waited for me until I finally decided to fully surrender to Him. He never stopped thinking of me. He thought of restoring and healing me so I can be whole, righteous and holy.

He thinks about me in the grandest and most mundane days of my years. He will think of me in the days to come until time is no more. His thoughts about me are countless and priceless.

I am no longer a nobody because my God defined my identity.

I am the princess of the King and precious are His thoughts about me.

PRECIOUS are your thoughts about me O God!

How great is the sum of them! Psalm 139:17

Devotion

Missing Piece

Have you had that misconception that a certain person, a position or a place can complete you?

We all have the yearning to find what seems to be missing in our lives. People have been searching for love everywhere, thinking that their lives will be complete when they finally find that dream. You think of a happily ever after with the man of your dreams. You can search for joy from your dream job. You can do everything to be noticed and accepted. You can strain eyeballs to get a promotion, or do everything to achieve your dream waistline and skin color. There is nothing wrong with that!

But the reality is, even if you end up with the man of your dreams, your knight in shining armor, your Mr. Right and man you have been praying for, you will realize that the love of this person you fought and prayed for isn't perfect. His love will fail in one way or the other. He will still disappoint you, offend you and hurt you because he is human and he makes mistakes.

Even if you reach the mountain top, the greener pastures or the land with milk and honey, they will never be enough to satisfy you. Even if you end up with your dream job, house and looks, they will never be enough to make you feel complete. They simply can't. There will always be a missing piece. Blais Pascal said, "There is a **God-shaped vacuum** in the heart of each man which cannot be satisfied by any created thing but only by **God** the Creator, made known through Jesus Christ."

There will always be seasons that we will long for solitude, a time with the ONE who truly loves us unconditionally. We will still yearn to rest in the arms of His everlasting love. There will always be a longing that only God can fill, pains that only He can heal, noise that only His voice can still.

"and you are complete in Him, who is the head of all principality and power." Colossians 2:10

All I desire is Christ

We all strive to become better individuals: gaining titles, working hard to be promoted and be recognized, striving to become good students/ parents/ friends/ employees/children, securing our future, fulfilling dreams, planning to live in a greener pasture, making wise investments, praying for good health, trying to make history, connecting to people and completing our bucket list. These are totally valid endeavors.

But there are quiet moments in our lives when we realize our utmost desire in life. It's the time that in our heart of hearts, we understood that everything else is useless and meaningless without Christ.

We find our greatest pleasure in sitting at His feet and gazing upon the beauty of His holiness and meditating in His presence. Everything else becomes rubbish compared to the highest privilege of knowing and experiencing His great love and faithfulness. In our inmost being we know that God is more than enough. I remember one of my grand mother's favorite songs, it says:

"Oh Lord, my God all I desire is You, Oh Lord, my God all I desire is You

More precious than silver, More costly than gold

No riches on the earth compares with You

And what can this world offer When all i desire is You?"

"What is more, I consider everything a loss because of the surpassing worth of knowing Christ Jesus my Lord, for whose sake I have lost all things. I consider them garbage, that I may gain Christ."

Philippians 3:8

Unharmed by fire

This season, I have been praying for several impossible things. Not just for myself, but most especially for the people I love: my family, friends, patients and students.

When I think of FIRE, I see two things: it can either BURN you or REFINE you. Shadrach, Meshack and Abednego walked around the fire unharmed. Though it was heated 7 times than usual, it did not touch them! There is no other god who can rescue like this!

Being a doctor was my ultimate dream. It was so hard achieving it, so when I finally got my license, I thought my life will be smooth sailing, I thought it will be a walk in the park. But I was wrong. I was surprised by the turn of events. My first paycheck was 120 Pesos gross, 60:40 split with the clinic. I had a toxic relationship, suffered hyper-obesity (BMI=57) and had depression. I finally got a good job but for some reason, I got bankrupt. I was a new doctor and it was so hard to survive. I held on to my faith and pleaded God for mercy and strength.

God did not leave me. His goodness chased me. He brought strangers to help me in my physical and emotional problems. He provided scholarships so I can specialize. He used the church to revive my emotional and spiritual life. He nourished my soul until he finally rescued me from the fire. My life was preserved. God gave back everything that was damaged: health, finances, emotions, relationships and my spiritual life.

What are you going through right now? Poor health, relational chaos, financial burden? Are you facing the giants, climbing a huge mountain, overcoming waves or walking through the valleys of death? Know that God can rescue you.

Nothing can harm you, not even a hair on your head will be singed, the fire will not touch you. The refining process will finish soon, and you will step out from the furnace unharmed. People around you will witness a miracle through your life. As you go through the fire, trust God. Hold on to God. He is with you.

I see four men, unbound, walking around in the fire unharmed! Daniel 3:25

Doorkeeper and an empty chair

I can work all day, all night; talk to students in the most unholy hour of the day about anything under the sun; teach pharma and biochemistry casually for all it's worth; brainstorm with competent workmates for big projects; travel to 3 different provinces in a week; see patients and befriend their loved ones; walk, laugh, cry and eat with the people I love. I can be sleep deprived and overworked doing these things over and over without getting exhausted because I just love doing each of them.

BUT NOTHING BEATS MY MOMENT WITH MY GOD.

I found myself sitting in a quiet and cozy place with good music, such a perfect place for a date. The empty chair in front of me is not a symbol of loneliness, deprivation or regret because I know God is sitting there. Conversation with the Lover of my soul is always the most refreshing of all conversations. His love lingers and His comfort is soothing. As songs started to overflow in my heart, I was humbled to realize that this God I worship has never left and never got tired of loving me. Whether I am obedient or stubborn; whether I am satisfied in Him or my heart is not right; both when it is easy or difficult to trust Him. In sickness, in health, in sorrow, in joy, in all-ness or in nothingness, He never left my side.

Even if my frail and fragile heart keeps on hurting Him, He remains faithful, unchanging and unfailing.

One day of intimacy with HIM is better than a thousand days without! I'd rather be a doorkeeper in the house of my beautiful God than to live my life without Him in the most beautiful palace elsewhere. Nothing could ever satisfy my heart like He does. NOTHING. NO ONE. I will always be at HOME in His presence.

For the Lord God is brighter than the brilliance of a sunrise! He wraps himself around me like a shield, He is generous with His gifts of grace. He provides all the needs of those who walk along His paths with integrity.

"Better is one day in your courts than a thousand elsewhere; I would rather be a doorkeeper in the house of my God than dwell in the tents of the wicked".

Psalm 84:10

How do you measure love?

Windows have special significance in my life. I had several encounters with the Lord as I look at windows.

Window of Miracle.

One humid morning in 2018, I was clueless on what life will bring. I was curious but not really expecting for an answer. But still I asked anyway, 'Lord, how do I measure your love?' Even I was ready for His silence, He gave me an unexpected answer as I glanced at the window.

I heard birds chirping and singing out loud in chorus with the wind blow. It was too humid but I felt the comforting cool breeze touching my face. The green leaves and grass are soothing to the eyes.

While enjoying the nature, I suddenly saw God's biggest surprise, my most awaited miracle and a delight to my heart. I didn't expect the answer to literally pass by.

I exclaimed, "God has never forgotten me." He said, "My child, I am always here. My silence doesn't mean I don't care. My love for you is constant. I see you, I hear you and I love you so dearly." More surprises started to take place, thereafter. There were pains and losses, but my 'miracle' remained and has always been God's reminder that His love will never fail.

———

Window of Love.

In 2019, my Mom opened her eyes, glanced at the window before she took her peaceful final breath. It's a picture of God's peace and comfort. I knew my Mom was ready to face Jesus. I knew, Jesus prepared my Mom for her glorious death.

———

Window of Hope.

In 2020, while I was sleeping in my migraine-inspired dark room, I was awoken by heavy rains. I opened my eyes and saw the window again. These past months have been an unpredictable journey of uncertainty. There is a huge temptation to entertain insecurity, loneliness, anxiety and apathy.

The window encourages me to look beyond the darkness that my eyes see. It may be raining outside but it showed me the beauty of the clouds, the melody of rainfall, the dancing branches of wet trees and the newness of the radiant morning. It opened up my sight to a brand-new day. It's another day to fight, to serve, to praise, to love and to see miracles.

The steadfast love of the Lord never ceases. His mercies never come to an end. They are new every morning, great is Thy faithfulness. Look beyond. Wait on God. You will see His surprises and miracles.

You will find reasons to hope again and rejoice again.

There, we will find pictures of God's immeasurable love.

My First, My Best and My All

Loving God is profound. We have many ways of loving Him and one of those is GIVING.

When we offer something to God, it should be our first and our best portion (not the leftovers). David showed an admirable example of that. He was offered a threshing place, oxen, yokes and boards for free. But He refused. Because He wanted His offering to cost him something. He gives God high reverence and he wanted to offer God nothing less than the best. That threshing place eventually became the place where God's temple was built! God truly honors our acts of worship through giving.

The *poor widow* in the new testament gave all that she had. She knew God deserves her all. God was pleased. The little boy offered his 5 loaves and 2 fish in John 6, then God multiplied it a thousand folds! In John 12, Mary poured a jar of expensive perfume on the feet of Jesus, wiping His feet with her hair and the house was filled with fragrance. That fragrance doesn't just define the perfume's value but also the depth of Mary's reverence to Jesus. God was pleased.

Giving is not limited to finances or material things. It could be quality time, talents, knowledge, skills and your very heart. There will be times that God will ask you to give and surrender all that you have, not to leave you empty-handed, but because He knows that in your emptiness, He can fill you with more. Obedience is the best form of worship. It's true that surrendering sometimes hurts. But the peace that it brings also heals.

I've been through a season of poverty few years back. Loans and expenses were beyond my monthly income that I can't even give my tithes. One day, God dealt with me to prioritize my tithes (10% of my salary). It was so hard to obey, because my salary was not even enough to pay for my bills. I talked to a Pastor (Hello Pastor Brandell!) and He told me that God will not bring me to a situation where His grace is not there. The next payday, I courageously set aside 10% of my income and dropped it in the tithe box and regularly did it until today. There was peace, I knew God was pleased.

Of course, it didn't end there. 6 months after that act of faith, for some miraculous reason, I was able to pay 80% of my loans, by God's sufficient grace. Amazing grace indeed! Few months later, I was officially debt-free. Praise God.

"I don't want to offer to the Lord my God burnt offerings that have cost me nothing".

2 Samuel 24:24

How can I not trust you, Lord?

Some battles come as a great surprise. We are caught unprepared and shocked, clueless on how to overcome and how to even survive. Seems all doors were shut; all jars are empty, and all efforts are futile. It's hard to find acceptable reasons why all battles come one after the other, and worst, they all happen when you are too weak to fight.

But pondering upon the life of JOSHUA gives encouragement.

After reading the famous chapter 1, and those chapters filled with names and tribes, it's amazing to know that despite all his limitations and inadequacies, he literally won every battle he faced (except for 1, I think) against BIG names and tribes! God fulfilled ALL His promises of victory to him. None of His promises failed.

And this made me think. How can we be afraid, when we know He has overcome the world?

How can we not trust God to supply all our needs, when we know that He owns the heaven and the earth? How can we not trust God to heal our diseases, when we know that He can actually raise up the dead to life again (Lazarus)? How can we not trust

God to give us wisdom, when we know He is all-knowing? How can we not trust God to fight for us, when He said, "the battle is mine?"

How can we not trust God to fix our relationships, when He is the God who can change hearts?

How can we not entrust to Him our lives, when He sent His Only Son to die on the cross because of His great love for us? How can we lose hope, when we know Jesus resurrected from the dead, promised to come back and share eternity with us?

How can we not trust this faithful God? Faithful to His words, faithful to his love, faithful to his promises.

"Not a single one of all the good promises the LORD *had given to the family of Israel was left unfulfilled; everything he had spoken came true". Joshua 21:45*

We need God

Whether you are a full-fledged doctor or an aspiring one.

A teacher or a student, a leader or a member, the CEO or the janitor, YOU NEED GOD

To whatever season in life you are in and whatever race you belong to, whether you're in north, in south, east or west, YOU NEED GOD.

In summer or in rainy days, in richness or in need, in sickness and in health, WE ALL NEED GOD.

In our exhaustion, He is our place of rest.

In our failed attempts, He rescues, revives and heals.

In our anxiety and insecurity, we can trust His Sovereignty.

In confusion and frustration, He is the Shepherd that leads His lambs.

In our dry and parched hearts, He is the Living Water who quenches thirst.

People leave and fail us.

Sometimes they reject and neglect us

They ignore and depreciate our value.

They choose not to choose us

In this broken and troubled world,

We are brainwashed that we should chase and beg for love.

But God...

He will never do that.

His love will always chase and choose us.

You never have to guess,

You never have to assume or expect anything less than what He says in His word.

He knows the number of our hair strands and how many times we blink our eyes.

He loves us completely and immeasurably.

He heals. He is not just thinking of the solution, He is the ultimate solution!

He specializes on impossibilities. He provides.

He answers prayers and gives hope.

He comforts and gives peace.

He directs and gives courage.

He makes us see things the way He does.

He makes us feel His heartbeat.

He wipes away our tears.

We're the apple of His eyes.

Our shortcomings will never intimidate God from loving and using us for His glory.

His love is free, full and complete. His love is unconditional, extravagant and perfect.

What an undeserved honor to have this solitude with Him where we can dance in the rhythm of His grace. In Him, we find real rest, delight and pleasure...

"Better is one day in your courts than a thousand elsewhere..." Psalm 84

Ultimate Source

Pastor Jonathan Ramirez once quoted, "We are channels of blessings, but God is the ultimate source of everything."

I can't help but remember the season when I was so broke. A young doctor whose expenses were far higher than her income; savings account was always on a red light; and I literally lived by faith every day for bills, gasoline and food.

But God created channels of blessings. Channels coming from family, friends and strangers. He surrounded me with people who gave me wise advice and helped me rise from the den. He taught me how to recognize and receive help from His ravens. Until I woke up one day, the 'storm' is already gone. The sun has shown up.

And as I look back, I know full well that it was God who made a way. He opened locked doors, filled empty barns and created a trail towards His 'supplies'. He protected me, provided for me and gave me peace. I understood full well that He made me go through those dark valleys so I can experience His refreshing springs as He clothe me with intangible blessings (Psalm 84)

We all have needs and valid reasons to worry. But we have a great Shepherd who cares for every detail of our lives.

James Hudson Taylor was right when he said, There are 3 stages to every great work:
first, IT IS IMPOSSIBLE; second, IT IS DIFFICULT; and third, IT IS DONE.

"I have been young and now I am old. And in all my years I have never seen the Lord forsake a man who loves him; nor have I seen the children of the godly go hungry."

Psalms 37:25

Di ako aalis dito

Sa buhay napakarami nating AKALA.
Akala mo eto na.
Akala mo yun na.
Akala mo SIYA NA.

At sa tuwing mapapatunayan mong mali ang akala mo, mapapailing ka nalang at magsasabing SAYANG. Sayang ang panahong inilaan, ang lakas na ibinuhos at mga luhang umagos.

Madami tayong SANA…
Sana hindi nalang ito ang ginawa ko, sana nakinig nalang ako, sana dati alam ko na ito, sana hindi nalang ito ang pinili ko.

Minsan dahil sa sobrang panghihinayang mo sa mga akalang di pala totoo, mga nasayang na oras na ngayon nama'y tila huminto. Mga 'sana' na nabigo at samu't saring mga dahilan para naisin mo nang sumuko.

Sigaw mo sa hangin, "Ayaw ko na ng ganito!"
Pero isipin mo minsan,

Kailangang MAWASAK ang plano mo para mabuo ang buhay mo.

May mga iginigiit tayo sa buhay na di talaga tugma sa Kanyang dakilang kalooban.

May mga anggulo na di mo masipat

At mga katotohanang Diyos lang ang makahahalungkat.

Minsan may mga lugar na dapat munang lisanin,

Mga salitang di muna dapat sabihin.

Mga yakap na di muna dapat gawin

At oras na dapat munang palipasin

Mga tao na dapat munang iwanan...

Hindi dahil masama kang kaibigan

Kundi dahil sa kanya-kanyang landas na inyong pupuntahan

Nais Niyang maransan mo ang Dakila Niyang KATAPATAN.

Sa pasilyong nilalakaran mo,

Sabi Niya sayo,

"Anak, ikaw muna at Ako."

"Di ako lumisan sa tabi mo,

Kahit kailan. pagtiwalaan Mo lang ako

Di Kita iiwan
Hayaan Mong maransan mo
Ang wagas na pag ibig Ko.
Dito lang ako sa tabi Mo,
Di ako aalis dito."

About the Author

The author is a Doctor of Medicine and Philosophy who specializes on Molecular and Clinical Nutrition. She is an Asst. Professor in Pharmacology in some medical schools in NCR and a manager in a multinational nutritional company. She is also a motivational speaker who finds great pleasure in caring for her students and patients; she has a heart to help build bridges and form the minds of the next generation. Tagalog is her mother tongue, she is a morning person, she laughs loud, and she loves to eat greens, fruits, eggs, cheesecake, *nata de coco* and dark chocolates. She is mostly quiet in a crowd but enjoys heart to heart conversations. She loves to play and talk to her nieces and nephews. Her interests include carpentry, music (opm/ papuri songs), poetry and nature.

www.ingramcontent.com/pod-product-compliance
Lightning Source LLC
LaVergne TN
LVHW041846070526
838199LV00045BA/1459